"If You Prete[nd...]
For The Wee[kend,...]
Presentation."

Conal Sutherland's eyes widened, as what she was saying finally registered. Livvy Farrell wanted him to spend the weekend pretending to be her fiancé. He would be able to kiss her and touch her to his heart's content, and if she objected, he could say that he was merely adding authenticity to his act. He'd long been thinking of ways to get her into bed, and now this gift from heaven had fallen into his lap. It seemed too good to be true, and that worried him.

"How am I supposed to behave?" he asked cautiously.

"Just be yourself."

"It's a deal." Conal fought to keep the triumph out of his voice.

"I didn't tell Mom that we were engaged, just that I was considering it," Livvy hurriedly corrected.

"Engaged is better. It gives us more leeway."

Dear Reader,

Hello! For the past few months I'm sure you've noticed the new (but probably familiar) name at the bottom of this letter. I was previously the senior editor of the Silhouette Romance line, and now, as senior editor of Silhouette Desire, I'm thrilled to bring you six sensuous, deeply emotional Silhouette Desire novels every month by some of the bestselling—and most beloved—authors in the genre.

January begins with *The Cowboy Steals a Lady*, January's MAN OF THE MONTH title and the latest book in bestselling author Anne McAllister's CODE OF THE WEST series. You should see the look on Shane Nichols's handsome face when he realizes he's stolen the wrong woman...especially when she doesn't mind being stolen or trapped with Mr. January one bit....

Wife for a Night by Carol Grace is a sexy tale of a woman who'd been too young for her handsome groom-to-be years ago, but is all grown up now.... And in Raye Morgan's *The Hand-Picked Bride*, what's a man to do when he craves the lady he'd hand-picked to be his brother's bride?

Plus, we have *Tall, Dark and Temporary* by Susan Connell, the latest in THE GIRLS MOST LIKELY TO... miniseries; *The Love Twin* by ultrasensuous writer Patty Salier; and Judith McWilliams's *The Boss, the Beauty and the Bargain*. All as irresistible as they sound!

I hope you enjoy January's selections, and here's to a very happy New Year (with promises of many more Silhouette Desire novels you won't want to miss)!

Regards,

Melissa Senate

Melissa Senate
Senior Editor

Please address questions and book requests to:
Silhouette Reader Service
U.S.: 3010 Walden Ave., P.O. Box 1325, Buffalo, NY 14269
Canadian: P.O. Box 609, Fort Erie, Ont. L2A 5X3

JUDITH McWILLIAMS
THE BOSS, THE BEAUTY AND THE BARGAIN

SILHOUETTE *Desire*®
Published by Silhouette Books
America's Publisher of Contemporary Romance

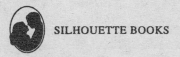

SILHOUETTE BOOKS

ISBN 0-373-76122-8

THE BOSS, THE BEAUTY AND THE BARGAIN

Books by Judith McWilliams

JUDITH McWILLIAMS

began to enjoy romances while in search of the proverbial "happily ever afters." But she always found herself rewriting the endings, and eventually the beginnings, of the books she read. Her husband finally suggested that she write novels of her own, and she's been doing so ever since. An ex-teacher with four children, Judith has traveled the country extensively with her husband and has been greatly influenced by those experiences. But while not tending the garden or caring for family, Judith does what she enjoys most—writing. She has also written under the name Charlotte Hines.

One

"Where have you been? It's two o'clock!"

Livvy Farrell pushed a damp strand of her black hair off her forehead and slipped out of her dripping raincoat, hanging it on the coatrack by the office door.

"You said you'd be back by one, and you were out in that downpour," Shawna accused.

Livvy grinned, her bright blue eyes brimming with laughter. "Ah, the ever-vigilant secretary. Nothing gets by you. Tell me, do I really want to know why you've developed a sudden interest in my whereabouts?"

"Probably not," Shawna said candidly. "This place has been like a zoo since you left. Your mother's phoned four times—and she sounds more desperate each time— that client with the building supply company has called you several times and the boss," Shawna nodded toward the oak door across from the reception room, "has been asking for you every five minutes." She grimaced. "I swear the man thinks I've got you locked in a closet somewhere.''

"Conal wants me?" Livvy felt a liquid warmth ooze through her at the thought of Conal Sutherland looking for her. Or better yet, of him finding her. Her finely drawn features unconsciously softened. He'd sweep her up in his powerful arms and crush her to his broad chest. Her internal temperature went up a few tenths of a degree just imagining what it would feel like to be pressed up against him.

It would feel fantastic, Livvy decided, absolutely fantastic. His dark brown eyes would gleam with suppressed passion, and he would murmur that he'd suddenly realized that he'd been looking for her all his life. That he couldn't wait to—

"Are you coming down with something?" Shawna demanded impatiently.

No, but I'd sure like to, Livvy thought ruefully. *Conal, to be specific. I'd like to pull him down into my bed and make mad, passionate love to him.*

Livvy made a determined effort to get her wayward imagination under control. She most emphatically didn't want Shawna to get the idea that she harbored any thoughts other than professional ones for Conal. The situation in their small office would become unbearable if Shawna were to decide to try to play matchmaker. Even worse, Conal might think that she'd put Shawna up to it. The appalling thought effectively squashed her ardor.

"What did Conal want?" Livvy asked.

Shawna shrugged. "I don't know. Neither of you ever tell me anything. Shall I let him know you're back?"

Livvy determinedly resisted the temptation. "No, first I'd better find out what's bothering my mother. Would you get her on the phone for me?"

Livvy went into her office, poured herself the last of the coffee in the pot and wearily sank into the brown leather chair behind her cluttered desk. She took a reviving sip of the concentrated caffeine and tried to wiggle the tension out of her shoulders caused by spending her lunch hour competing with other equally harried shoppers.

When the phone rang, she put the coffee cup down on one of the reasonably level piles of paper and answered it.

"Livvy, the most awful thing has happened!" Her mother didn't even bother with a perfunctory hello. "The restaurant I hired to cater the food for your grandparents' fiftieth anniversary party had a kitchen fire and is out of business for the foreseeable future!" Marie's voice rose to a wail. "What am I going to do?"

"Calm down for starters," Livvy automatically slipped into her soothing-the-nervous-client mode. "I will admit it's aggravating, but—"

"'Aggravating'!" Marie squawked.

"Very aggravating," Livvy amended, "but it's nothing that can't be overcome."

"Every other caterer in Scranton is already booked for the weekend. And your Aunt Rose wasn't the least bit of help. She just kept saying that because I was the oldest, I ought to do it."

"Mmm," Livvy murmured, realizing that her mother didn't want advice, she wanted sympathy. Something Livvy was more than willing to provide. After all, her mother really did have a right to gripe about the way her sisters had dumped the organizing of their parents' anniversary reunion entirely on her shoulders. Although if it were left up to her scatterbrained aunt Rose, the whole family would sit down to peanut butter sandwiches. Her grandparents deserved better than that. They merited the very best their family could arrange, Livvy thought on a wave of love.

"And the trouble I had finding a baker who was willing to copy the wedding cake Mom and Dad had. No one wants to tackle anything the least bit out of the ordinary these days," Marie said, continuing her litany of woes. "The only thing I can think to do at this point is to have everyone pitch in and bring food. There are far too many people coming for one person to make everything."

"Sounds reasonable," Livvy responded, wondering what it would be like to have been married for that long. Her eyes narrowed thoughtfully as she tried to imagine Conal as her husband of fifty years. She couldn't because her mind was too busy envisioning him as a bridegroom. His dark brown hair would have a thin coating of silvery confetti from the wedding party, and his eyes would be aglow with passion. He would— Her imagination faltered under the strain of trying to picture Conal saying, "I do." Not when he'd already been so vocal about the fact that he wouldn't.

Livvy stifled a sigh. The only place Conal was likely to be a bridegroom was in her dreams.

"But I do have good news, too."

Livvy's finely honed sense of self-preservation kicked in at the nervous tremor in her mother's voice.

"What's that?" Livvy asked cautiously.

"I was talking to Teresa next door who said that her husband's second cousin's son is staying with them, and he doesn't have anything planned for this weekend."

"So?"

Marie gave a long suffering sigh as if she despaired of her daughter's intelligence and said, "This weekend is your grandparents' party."

"I know that. I just spent my entire lunch hour and another hour besides finding the perfect gift for them."

"It means that he can be your date for the weekend." Marie refused to be sidetracked.

"No," Livvy said flatly.

"He's willing to do it," Marie assured her. "Teresa asked him, and he said he didn't have anything better to do."

"He may be willing, but I'm not," Livvy said, having had far too many visits home ruined by Marie's unquenchable desire to see her youngest daughter married off.

"But, Livvy, if you don't do it, I'll have to listen to your grandma lecture me about what a disgrace it is that you're almost thirty and still not married. And if your aunt May makes one more crack about how sad it is that with all the millions of men in New York City, not one of them is willing to marry you..." Marie's voice trembled.

Livvy bit back an acid rejoinder about what her aunt May could do with her pseudo sympathy. She didn't care what the family thought about her single state, but she knew her mother did. Marie cared very much.

"Mom, I really—"

"It's just for the weekend," Marie said hurriedly. "And Teresa says that he's really a nice boy. He just fell in with bad company and—"

Boy? Bad company? Livvy shuddered. It seemed that the closer she got to thirty the less exacting Marie's requirements in a prospective son-in-law were becoming, but it really sounded as if this one had been dredged up from the bottom of the barrel, literally.

"No," Livvy said, breaking into Marie's obviously rehearsed recitation. "Absolutely not."

To Livvy's horror, her mother burst into tears. "It's

just for the weekend,'' Marie sobbed. ''What's one weekend, and it'll at least prove to everyone that you can get a date. Please, dear, do it for me?''

''I can't because...because I've already asked someone home for the party.'' Livvy blurted out the first excuse that came to mind.

''What?'' Marie's tears miraculously disappeared. ''Why didn't you say anything before?''

''Because he hasn't accepted yet,'' Livvy improvised. ''He said he'd let me know if he can clear his calendar.''

''He sounds very important,'' Marie said approvingly. ''I can't believe that after years of my telling you to grab one of those executives in New York, you've actually done it. What does he do, dear?''

''He's in advertising like me,'' Livvy mumbled.

''But what if he can't come?'' Marie worried. ''Maybe we ought to hold the one I found in reserve just in case.''

''No!''

''But—''

''I can't date anyone else, Mom.'' Livvy groped for a reason that sounded plausible. She could hardly tell her mother that she felt disloyal dating other men because she was fixated on a man who viewed marriage as a specialized form of indentured servitude. Somehow it seemed the final irony that after avoiding marriage for years while she got her career firmly launched, she had finally fallen in love with, and wanted to marry, a man who seemed to want no part of the institution. From various comments he'd made, it was clear Conal didn't intend to let any woman occupy a meaningful role in his life.

Deciding that if she were going to take up lying, she might as well go for the big time, Livvy closed her eyes and announced, ''He's asked me to marry him, and I haven't decided whether I want to or not.''

"Marry!"

Livvy winced at the ecstatic sound in Marie's voice. Her mother hadn't sounded that happy since her sister Fern had given birth to her only grandchild. Her mother was going to be very let down when Livvy arrived for the party by herself and told her that she'd refused her imaginary suitor.

"Listen, Mom, I've got to run. I've got a million and one things that need to be done."

"Of course, dear. I can hardly wait to meet your Prince Charming."

"Prince Charming doesn't exist. He's just a man. Bye." Livvy hurriedly hung up before Marie asked any more questions, such as the name of her mythical suitor.

Livvy took another sip of the tepid coffee, feeling like an ungrateful daughter. But a determined, ungrateful daughter. Not even to please her mother was she willing to spend the weekend trying to fend off the neighbor's husband's second cousin's boy. Who had "just fallen in with bad company." Livvy shuddered. Besides, with any luck at all Marie would be so busy with all the visiting relatives that she wouldn't have time to focus too much on Livvy's failure to produce a fiancé.

The sudden ringing of the phone startled her, and Livvy jumped, spilling coffee down the front of her cream silk blouse. She frowned at the dark, spreading patch in exasperation. That was all the afternoon needed to complete it. A stain on her brand-new blouse.

The phone rang again, and Livvy picked it up. She identified herself and then wished she hadn't when she recognized the voice of Walt Larson, a client who had hired their advertising agency to design a campaign to promote his building supply company.

"You were wrong, Miss Farrell," Larson announced gleefully.

Firmly walling her annoyance behind the practical demands of keeping the customer happy, Livvy forced a laugh. "It would hardly be the first time, Mr. Larson. But what exactly are you referring to?"

"I checked, and it isn't against the law to have a big-breasted woman in a tiny bikini in a television ad."

"It's against the law of good taste!" Livvy's resolve slipped slightly. "Mr. Larson, you sell building supplies for the do-it-yourselfer. What do scantily clad women have to do with that?"

"Sex sells!" he insisted. "You're supposed to be the advertising expert. You should know that."

Livvy gritted her teeth, counted to ten and then said, "That is a gross oversimplification."

"Now you listen to me, Miss Farrell...." Livvy turned at the sound of a sharp knock on her door. Before she could respond, it was pushed open. Larson's hectoring voice faded to a minor annoyance in the background, as Conal's large body filled her vision. Eagerly her eyes skimmed over his face. His dark eyes gleamed with suppressed excitement, sending a wave of anticipation through her.

Her eyes instinctively sought the intriguing line of his mouth, lingering over the firmness of his lips. She didn't know what had excited him, but she sure knew what would work for her—if he were to gather her in his arms and press his lips to hers. A shiver raced over her skin, raising goosebumps.

"...pay the bills!" Larson's indignant tone finally registered in Livvy's bemused mind.

"Yes, Mr. Larson, but..." Her concentration suffered a major setback when Conal perched on the edge of her desk, and Larson launched back into his tirade. She could feel the warmth from his large body reaching out to her. Luring her closer to him.

In self-defense she dropped her eyes and found herself staring at his thigh. His muscles were pushing against the thin gray material of his suit pants, and Livvy felt her fingers tremble with the urge to touch him. To probe the strength of his muscles and find out if they were as hard as they looked. To—

"...big boobs," Larson concluded.

"Boobs!" Livvy jerked up, outrage momentarily dousing her fascination with Conal's body.

"Breasts," Conal amended in a stage whisper.

Livvy ignored him, even if she couldn't entirely ignore the tightening of her own breasts at the gleam of mischief in Conal's eyes. Clients might be important, but there were limits to what she was willing to do to keep an account. Larson was skating seriously close to that limit.

Livvy's eyes narrowed as an idea suddenly occurred to her.

"Mr. Larson, I will concede that you have a point that sex sells, but you're being very unimaginative about it. Instead of a bikini-clad woman, why don't we hire a model from one of the male strip clubs?"

"What?" Larson sounded confused.

"It'll be great," Livvy said blandly. "We can get a muscular type in a sequined jockstrap and—"

"You can't do that!" Mr. Larson sputtered.

"Why not?" Livvy felt the trembling of Conal's body, and she looked up to see him choking on the laughter he was trying to contain. Conal would be a natural in the role, she thought dreamily. They could put him in a red-sequined bit of nothing and drape him over a power saw.

Her eyes narrowed thoughtfully. She would buy. And so would half the women in New York City.

"I don't think you appreciate my business," Larson blustered. "I've half a mind to take it elsewhere."

Half a mind about summed it up, Livvy thought acidly. "We would be very sorry to loose your business," she lied, "but of course you must do what you think best."

She gently hung up the phone in contrast to the way Larson slammed the receiver down.

"What was that all about?" Conal asked.

"Inappropriate sex," Livvy muttered, not wanting to talk about Larson's fixation with large-breasted women.

"Sex inappropriate? Is that possible in this culture?" Conal grinned at her, his white teeth gleaming darkly against his tanned face, and the laugh lines around his eyes deepening. When he smiled, he smiled with his whole face, Livvy realized. Would he make love with the same intensity? Would he— Stop it. Livvy hastily yanked her imagination up short. She absolutely had to get some kind of grip on her daydreams, because they were beginning to take over her mind every time she even thought about Conal. Somehow she had to find a way to dilute her fascination with him because time wasn't doing it, as she'd hoped it would when she'd first met him eighteen months ago. Time only seemed to be deepening her attraction to him.

She took a deep, steadying breath and said, "Forget our probably ex-client and tell me what happened."

Conal shifted uneasily. He momentarily couldn't remember why he'd come into her office in the first place. He'd taken one look at the aggravation on her face, and had wanted nothing more than to take her in his arms and wipe away every last vestige of strain. He wanted to kiss her until he managed to replace her annoyance with the mindless bliss of sexual desire. He stared down into the brilliant blue of her eyes, desperately wanting to see them grow cloudy with passion. Passion for him.

He clenched his teeth against the burgeoning need that shot through him like a pain. Fat chance he had of that, he thought grimly. He couldn't even convince her to go out with him, let alone go to bed with him. Patience. He repeated what had become his mantra during the long months Livvy had worked for him. Sooner or later he was bound to find a chink in her armor. If he was ever to convince Livvy to see him as her lover, he absolutely couldn't do anything to scare her off. As long as he remained on friendly terms with her, he would be in a position to take advantage of it. In the meantime he would tell her the good news.

"I got a phone call from Grandma Betty's Soup Company."

Livvy sat up in sudden interest. As far as she knew, it was the first time they'd been approached by a subsidiary of one of the large multinational chains.

"And?" Livvy prodded him.

"And they want us to submit a proposal for a new line of soup mixes they're developing." He offered the words like a gift.

"That's fantastic!" Livvy enthused.

"It sure is. To paraphrase someone or other, this could be the start of something big."

But not too big. Livvy instinctively rejected the thought of Conal expanding his small agency. She loved working closely with him and wouldn't want to lose that intimacy.

"There's just one thing," Conal added slowly as he reached the part that he knew was going to be tricky.

"As long as it doesn't involve bikinis, I can deal with it."

"It's the time element. From the deadline they set for our first presentation, I think they originally tried another ad agency and it didn't work out."

"How tight is the timing?"

"They want a presentation in six weeks."

"Six weeks! It's impossible. Have you forgotten my vacation starts Friday?"

"Take it later," Conal suggested.

"This is later. I was supposed to go in August and had to postpone it when we had that rush job for the record chain. Besides, I've already made reservations in Extaca." Livvy stiffened her resolve not to give in. She had deliberately planned her vacation in Mexico, hoping that being so far away from Conal would allow her to get her obsession under control. But even so, Conal was right. This really was a great opportunity. An opportunity she would normally have grabbed with both hands.

"You're tense." Conal watched the line between her eyebrows deepen in indecision. "That fool Larson has upset you. You have to learn to ignore people like him."

"That comes under the heading of easier said than done." Livvy made no attempt to correct his misapprehension. "I..."

Her thoughts scattered like dry leaves in a gale-force wind when Conal stepped behind her and placed his large hands on her shoulders. She could feel the weight of them pressing against her.

"Relax." Conal's deep voice was a soothing murmur that lapped seductively against her tense muscles. "Just blank out your mind and allow yourself to drift." His fingers closed around the slim bones of her shoulders, and he rubbed his thumbs over her silk-clad skin.

Livvy instinctively took a deep breath, sucking in the provocative fragrance of his cologne. He smelled delicious. Like— She shivered as he suddenly slipped his fingers beneath her collar and massaged the base of her neck. A heavy weight seemed to be pulling her eyelids down. His touch felt so good. So right.

Feeling greatly daring, she leaned her head back against his chest. It felt hard. Intriguingly hard.

"There." Conal's voice sounded deeper than usual as he stepped back, and she wondered if it was a result of him touching her. Could he have found it exciting? It was a heady thought, even if she had her doubts about it.

Livvy watched as Conal began to pace. Not an easy thing to do in her small office. His face was set in hard lines, and there was a determined jut to his square jaw. A wave of tenderness at his purposeful expression shook her.

"Why don't you do the proposal yourself?" she suggested. "You don't really need me." She ignored the quick flash of pain her words caused.

Conal shoved his long fingers through his short brown hair in frustration. "I can't do it. They were very specific about wanting a light touch for the campaign. Along the lines of that whimsical thing you did for Ebbings Bakery. I simply don't have your humorous flair."

Despite her misgivings, Livvy was unable to resist the glow of pleasure his compliment gave her. They really did make a great team. They each had a skill the other lacked. Which was all the more reason not to ruin the ideal working relationship with a short-term personal one, she reminded herself. Because while an affair with Conal would be fantastic, it wouldn't last. Relationships held together strictly by sex never did. And while she might love Conal with all her heart, he certainly didn't love her. Eventually the pleasure of making love to her would become commonplace for Conal and he would end their affair, leaving a lot of memories and possible resentments between them that would be bound to interfere with a working relationship. She would have no choice but to leave. And then she would have nothing. Not Conal and not her job. Nothing but memories, and she was far too young to be living on memories.

"But I've already made reservations," Livvy repeated doggedly, hoping she sounded more enthusiastic than she felt. The prospect of two weeks in Mexico paled next to the thought of spending the time working closely with Conal on the proposal.

"Cancel them. Think of the agency. Think of the future."

I am, Livvy thought grimly. *The future of my peace of mind.* And the very faint hope that if she weren't around for two weeks Conal might suddenly realize how much he missed her. Might begin to question his aversion to marriage.

"Think of the fact that I'll owe you a favor," he added.

A favor? Livvy stared into his gleaming eyes and felt her insides twist in sudden desire. She could think of several favors that she would like from him, starting with a long kiss and ending with her naked body wrapped in his arms. He would be—

Livvy blinked as she was suddenly struck with a blinding flash of inspiration. She sat up straighter as the idea began to gel in her mind.

She had told her mother that she was bringing home a date for the weekend. A man who had asked her to marry him. What if she were to ask Conal to pretend to be that man in exchange for her canceling her vacation and doing his soup proposal? Her eyes narrowed thoughtfully. Not only would it temporarily relieve the pressure of her mother's constant nagging about finding a husband, but also, with Conal pretending to be her almost fiancé, the opportunity might well come up to kiss him. Or even make love to him. Her stomach twisted longingly at the thought. This could be her chance to explore her feelings for Conal without having to worry about repercussions, because Conal would think her every response was nothing more than an act. He wouldn't realize how much it meant to her. Maybe if she were able to make love to him, she would realize that it wasn't such a big deal. Maybe her fascination with him was nothing more than a variation of the "forbidden fruit" idea. Or maybe, if fortune were really smiling on her, Conal would like being engaged to her so much he would want to make it permanent.

Livvy swallowed a sigh, knowing the chances of that happening were almost nil. During that time she'd been working closely with him, his attitude toward marriage hadn't softened one iota. Nor had she been able to find out why he was against it. It wasn't as if he led a wild, swinging lifestyle that marriage could interfere with.

There was so much she didn't know, when it came to Conal. A sense of discouragement weighed her down. If she had any common sense, she would quit. She would find another job and another man to love. Someone who wasn't averse to commitment. Perhaps if she weren't seeing Conal every day, other men would begin to look more interesting.

She placated her common sense, telling it *later*. She had time. She wasn't even thirty yet. She could afford to indulge her dreams of Conal awhile yet, before she had to start worrying about her biological clock running down.

"A huge favor," Conal upped the ante.

Livvy stared at him, torn between hope and fear of rejection. What did she have to lose by asking him? She tried to consider the situation logically. Since he didn't know she had an emotional reason for wanting him to agree, she was no worse off than before if he said no.

But if he were to agree... She shivered beneath the sudden onslaught of sensation that blossomed in her chest. If he agreed, anything might happen.

"There is something you could do for me," Livvy said slowly, trying to figure out the best way to say it. "This weekend is my grandparents' fiftieth wedding anniversary, and my mother is organizing a family reunion for the event. All the relatives will be there."

"I always wanted to belong to a big family when I was a kid."

Livvy grimaced at his wistful tone. "Believe me, the reality leaves a lot to be desired...which brings me to my problem. While I dearly love my family, I don't agree with the older members on a lot of issues, and one of them is about a woman's place in the general scheme of things. They think that a woman's first priority in life should be catching a husband, and her last should be keeping him happy. Careers are something men have."

"Thereby assuring herself of a meal ticket for life," he said.

"You obviously haven't seen the divorce statistics lately." This time Livvy tried challenging one of his derogatory comments about marriage instead of simply ignoring them the way she normally did. A feeling of satisfaction filled her as Conal blinked in surprise at her tart words. Obviously her response had caught him off guard. Now to try to keep him off guard.

"The problem is that my mother is determined to marry me off before I turn thirty next month," she continued slowly.

Conal grinned at her. "I can see her point. It's all

downhill for a woman after thirty, while a man is just coming into his prime.''

''I suggest you keep your cracks to yourself or you'll never live to see your prime!

''To get back to my problem, the situation has gotten so bad that my mother just called to tell me that she had arranged a blind date for me for the weekend.''

Conal tensed, trying to suppress the spurt of anger that suffused him at the thought of Livvy going out with another man.

''I told my mother no, and when she started to cry, I got flustered. I said I couldn't date him because I was thinking of marrying someone else, and I was bringing him home for the weekend.''

Conal felt a jagged shard of some dark emotion lacerate his composure. He hadn't known that she was dating anyone, let alone considering marriage. Although he'd known from the first moment he'd seen her that sooner or later she probably would marry. Livvy was everything a man wanted in a woman, if a wife was what he wanted. Which he didn't, he reminded himself. Marriage and kids were not for him. He'd settled that question long ago. Or rather it had been settled for him, he thought grimly.

''Do I know him?'' Conal was relieved to hear the even tone of his voice. He didn't dare let her know that he cared one way or the other. To do so would be to run the risk of losing what little he did have of her. If she were to start to feel uncomfortable around him, she would leave, and he wouldn't be able to see her every morning. He wouldn't ever hear that funny little gurgle of laughter she gave when something really amused her. He wouldn't have her around to listen to his ideas and offer insightful suggestions.

Livvy sighed. "There isn't anyone. I just said that to stop Mom from crying."

Conal felt himself sag as an overwhelming feeling of relief washed through him, loosening his rigid muscles. He felt as if a benevolent fate had just lifted the weight of the world off his shoulders.

"So if you would agree to come with me this weekend and pretend to be the man—" Livvy paused and then blurted out "—who has asked me to marry him, I'll postpone my vacation and do the soup presentation for you."

Conal's eyes widened as what she was saying finally registered. Livvy wanted him to spend the weekend pretending to be her fiancé? A feeling of exultation filled him. He would be able to kiss her and touch her to his heart's content, and if she objected, he could say that he was merely trying to add authenticity to his act. Since the first moment he'd laid eyes on her, he'd been trying to figure out a way to get her into bed, and now this gift from heaven had fallen into his lap. It seemed too good to be true, and that worried him. Things that seemed too good to be true usually were. He pushed his sense of pleasure aside and tried to find the fly in the ointment.

"How am I supposed to behave?" he asked cautiously.

"Just be yourself," Livvy said, beginning to relax slightly at his matter-of-fact response. "You see, my mom is always telling me that I should grab one of the rising young executive types that frequent the street corners of New York City."

"Those are not the types who frequent street corners in New York City!"

Livvy shrugged. "I know it, and you know it, but Mom is convinced it's true. Anyway, I think if she were to actually meet a high-powered executive type she wouldn't be so keen to see me married to one."

Conal chuckled. "I think I've just been insulted."

"Not really. It's just that Mom's idea of a perfect husband is a man like my father was. He worked his shift at the mine and spent his evenings and weekends at home with his family. In fact, according to Mom, the only disobliging thing he ever did was to get himself killed while she was pregnant with me," Livvy said wryly.

"I see," Conal said slowly, wondering if that was also Livvy's idea of a perfect man. Was that why she had refused all his invitations? Because she wanted a stolid, unimaginative man who never took any risks. It was a depressing thought, but he refused to dwell on it. Right now he needed to concentrate on his unexpected opportunity to show her how great they could be together. To prove to her that the factors that made them mesh so well in the office would work equally well in bed.

"It's a deal." Conal fought to keep his sense of triumph out of his voice. "I'll masquerade as your fiancé and you'll do the presentation."

"I didn't tell Mom that we were engaged, just that I was considering it," Livvy hurriedly corrected him.

"Engaged is better. It gives us more leeway. Tell me what kind of engaged couple we're supposed to be," he said before she could question what sort of leeway he meant. "Is this a Bertie Wooster type of engagement, where I call you 'old girl' and pat you on the shoulder?"

"You like Jeeves and Wooster, too?" Livvy asked, momentarily diverted.

"I bought the entire set of videos when I was in England last spring. If you do a good job on the presentation, I'll let you watch them. But to get back to our discussion. If it isn't a Bertie Wooster type of engagement, is it like one of those old Doris Day, Rock Hudson movies from the sixties? The kind where he kisses her like this."

To Livvy's dumbfounded amazement, Conal leaned down and pressed his lips to hers. The scent of his cologne was stronger that close to him, and it caused the bottom to drop out of her stomach.

To her disappointment he straightened up almost immediately and stared down into her eyes.

"Somehow that doesn't seem quite right," he said slowly.

Livvy ran the tip of her tongue over her bottom lip and stared into his eyes. There was a light glittering in their depths that she wished was passion but feared was simply devilment.

"I can't quite see you as Doris Day. You're more the foreign-film type of heroine."

"I am?" she asked weakly, still off balance from his unexpected kiss.

"Uh-huh. Full of unfathomable secrets and hidden purposes."

He cupped the back of her head with his large hand and pressed his lips against her mouth. His tongue darted out to lick over her bottom lip and Livvy shivered, instinctively opening her mouth. He immediately took advantage and began to explore with his tongue inside. Livvy trembled at its rough texture, and her hands came up to clutch his arms. She felt as if she needed an anchor in a world that had suddenly lost all its familiar moorings.

Her fingers slipped over the crisp cotton of his shirt, digging into the muscles below. Kissing him was turning out to be every bit as fantastic as she'd imagined it would be.

Livvy bit back her instinctive protest as he raised his head and stared down into her flushed face. Kissing him was also filled with potential pitfalls, she reminded herself. She absolutely had to keep her wits about her when she was around him. No matter how hard it was.

"I was right. You are definitely the foreign-film type," Conal murmured, and his warm breath wafted across her cheeks making the skin tighten.

Livvy stared up at him, wondering what she had let herself in for. Nothing she couldn't handle, she told herself, trying hard to believe it.

Two

Livvy tensed as the doorbell shattered the stillness in her apartment. Its normally melodious chimes suddenly seemed raucous. Nervously she ran her turquoise silk pullover down over her faded jeans. Conal was here! But that wasn't any reason to be jittery, she tried to tell herself. She had never felt nervous around him before. Exasperated, sometimes, and usually excited, but never just plain nervous.

But then she'd never been pretending to be his fiancée. The thought sent a flood of complex emotions swirling through her, the major one being anticipation.

The bell chimed again. After quickly glancing around her small living room to make sure that she hadn't inadvertently left out one of the numerous portraits of Conal in various stages of undress that she had painted over the last year and a half, Livvy hurried to open it.

The sight of Conal standing there wearing a pair of tan

slacks and an Aran knit sweater momentarily left her speechless. He looked even larger in the bulky sweater than he normally did. And somehow different in casual clothes.

"Good afternoon," Livvy said, feeling awkward. Their pretend engagement had introduced a new element into their relationship. An element she didn't quite feel comfortable with yet.

"Not so far it hasn't been!" Conal stalked into her apartment.

Livvy blinked, caught off guard by his scowl. Was he regretting their masquerade already? Did he want to back out of their agreement?

"Larson stopped by the office this afternoon right after you left," Conal announced. "He brought the model he hired with him to see what you thought."

"And to think I missed a treat like that," Livvy said, relaxing slightly when she realized that Conal's ill humor was work related.

"You probably would have thought it was a treat," Conal said sourly, "since you were the one who gave him the bright idea."

"I did not! I am intellectually and morally opposed to the exploitation of the female body by a bunch of overage, drooling male adolescents!"

Conal's annoyance dissolved in the face of her outraged expression. "Very good. Did you practice that or does such slogan mongering come naturally?"

"I am not kidding," Livvy muttered. "I think it's disgraceful."

"I agree with you, but you've got the wrong end of the stick. Larson thought about what you said about finding some overmuscled male to wear a sequined jockstrap in the commercial and decided it was a great idea."

Livvy's mouth fell open, and she stared at Conal in shock. "He found a male model in a red sequined jockstrap?"

"Actually they were blue sequins," Conal said. "And I couldn't talk him out of it."

"I should hope not!" Livvy said virtuously. "Total nudity is going entirely too far."

"Where's your sense of outrage now?" Conal demanded.

"I'm looking for it."

"Well, you'd better find it before Monday morning because Larson is coming back."

Livvy grinned. "Lovely...something to look forward to. Maybe he'll bring the model with him. I've never actually seen a sequined jockstrap."

And if he had his way she never would, Conal thought on a flash of a dark, uncomfortable emotion that he very much feared was jealousy. He didn't want Livvy looking at strange men. For that matter he didn't want her looking at familiar men. At least not until he'd had a chance to thoroughly explore the emotions she seemed to so effortlessly raise in him. Explore them and dissipate them. Then he wouldn't mind what she did.

"Where's your suitcase?" Livvy suddenly realized that he hadn't brought one. A feeling of disappointment engulfed her. Had her first guess been right, after all? Had he changed his mind about pretending to be her fiancé?

"I left it in the car," he murmured, trying to decide if this would be a good time to give her the diamond he'd spent all last evening choosing or whether he should wait until they had actually arrived at her home. Now, he decided. That way if she objected he would be able to argue with her, something he couldn't do in front of her family.

He'd wanted to buy her a piece of jewelry for months

now. Something like a diamond pendant. On a long gold chain so that the diamond would nestle between her breasts. Her bare breasts. He swallowed at the tantalizing image that popped into his mind. Later, he told himself. When they were actually lovers, he would buy her what he wanted. But for now he would have to be satisfied with giving her what he could make a good case for her accepting.

Conal pulled the small black leather box out of his pant's pocket and shoved it at her.

"Here," he said. "To help the impersonation."

Livvy stared at the box as a feeling of longing, heavily tinged with sadness, slipped through her. It had to be an engagement ring. An engagement ring she wanted so desperately to be real. A ring she wanted to mean something to him. To be a promise from him for a future together.

Livvy took the box and slowly opened it. A gasp escaped her as the huge diamond caught the sunlight pouring in through the window and splintered it into a million fragments of rainbow-colored light. The ring was absolutely gorgeous in its simplicity. A single stone set in a plain gold band. It practically shouted good taste and…the money to indulge it, she realized. Anything that beautifully cut, to say nothing of that big, had to have cost a fortune. She couldn't accept it. Even temporarily. No matter how much she wanted to. It was far too valuable.

"If you don't like it—"

"It's the most gorgeous ring that I've ever seen," she said truthfully.

"Then what's the problem?"

"What if I lost it?" she asked.

"I'd collect from my insurance company. It's just a ring I bought a few years ago and then didn't need," he lied. Somehow, it was very important to him that she accept that ring. Accept it and wear it.

"A few years ago?" Livvy tried to swallow the metallic taste of anger that unexpectedly coated her mouth. Why had he been so willing to marry some other woman then and yet he was now vocally opposed to marriage?

"Uh-huh. There was this gorgeous blonde..." Conal tried to lull her suspicions.

"Why is it always a blonde?" Livvy snapped, not wanting to hear about the woman who had almost tempted Conal into marriage despite his clear aversion to the state. Or had it been the blonde who had soured him on marriage?

"It isn't always a blonde," Conal assured her. "There was a redhead named Cindy, who—"

"That was a rhetorical question," she cut him off. "Not a request for a list of your conquests."

Conal grinned ruefully. "I think I was Cindy's conquest if you want the truth. But fascinating as you appear to find my past love life, we need to get going. According to the rental agent, it'll take us a good three hours to get to Scranton at this time of day."

"A bad three hours. The traffic is always miserable." Livvy stalled, suddenly overwhelmed by last-minute doubts about the wisdom of changing the status quo. She had the strangest feeling that once she put on Conal's ring nothing would ever be the same again, and she was afraid. She might find her hopeless love for Conal emotionally frustrating, but she could handle it. Once she got a taste of what it was like to be physically close to him, could she handle the deprivation which would fill her when they returned to New York and he slipped back into his old role as her boss?

"Sorry, what am I thinking of? I almost forgot."

Livvy looked up at Conal, wondering what he was talking about. She wasn't left wondering for long. He grabbed her and pulled her up against his chest. His arms tightened around her, squashing her against him. A hot, tingling sensation sizzled through her breasts leaving them achy. She wanted nothing more than to close her eyes and savor the sensation. Instead, she forced herself to focus on what he'd said.

"Forgot what?" she mumbled into his sweater.

"That we're supposed to be an engaged couple. Engaged couples kiss."

Engaged couples do lots of things, Livvy thought longingly, as a sudden image of Conal's broad, bare shoulders filled her mind.

Livvy fought against the desire that was eating at her composure and tried to think. It was hopeless. The only thing she could think about was what it felt like to be pressed up against him. Even better than she'd thought it would.

She peered up into his eyes. There were tiny sparks glowing deep in them. Like minuscule explosions of passion were being set off just below the surface. But was it really passion? And if it was, was his passion directed at her personally or was it simply the result of him holding a woman, and any woman would have produced the same results?

The question lost some of its urgency as she watched his head come closer. Her breath caught in her throat as she stared at his firm lips. They looked so enticing. So alluring. She wanted to taste them and explore the exact shape and texture of them.

Her eyelids were becoming heavy, weighted down by her growing need. It was all she could do not to grab his head and yank him down to her. Finally when she was ready to scream with frustration, his lips brushed hers and a shower of reaction drenched her. Goose bumps popped up on her arms, and shivers chased after them. To her massive disappointment Conal made no effort to deepen their kiss. Instead, he raised his head, staring down at her, his expression unreadable.

What was he thinking? Unease began to nudge aside the pleasure Livvy felt. Had he found their kiss a disappointment? Chagrin drove the last lingering shreds of desire from her mind. The thought that Conal might find her deficient in the area of lovemaking made her feel confused and uncertain. Her relationship with him to date might not have developed along the lines she'd wanted, but at least it had been fairly clear and uncomplicated. It hadn't reduced her to this present dithering mass of uncertainty.

Livvy watched as Conal took her hand and gently pushed the ring over her finger. It was a perfect fit. An omen? All it signified was that the girlfriend that Conal had bought it for had the same size hands she did. She mentally chided herself. The idea that she was nothing more than one of an interchangeable line of women moving through his life infuriated her.

"Thanks," she snapped, and turned to her suitcase, which was sitting open on the sofa.

Conal frowned slightly at her clipped tone, wondering if it was the ring she objected to or if the problem was with the man who had placed it on her finger. Or could it simply be that she was nervous about the coming weekend? He didn't know. There was so much he didn't know, he thought uneasily. Starting with how to act around her family. His experience with families was limited to visits to his married friends and what he'd seen on television. He wasn't so naive as to believe that sitcom characters represented reality. At least he sure hoped not.

Concentrate on what you can do and don't worry about what you can't, Conal reminded himself of the motto he'd shaped his life around. He had finally managed to breach Livvy's seemingly impenetrable professional shield. Or rather, her mother had breached it for him. But whatever the reason, he now had the opportunity to get to know Livvy on a personal basis.

Conal swallowed as his body clenched beneath the on-slaught of images he had of just how personally he would like to get to know her. He wanted so much to take her in his arms again. To nuzzle the velvety skin of her cheek. To run his lips down over the soft flesh of her neck. To explore the precise texture of her breasts. To... He took a deep, steadying breath. For so long he'd felt starved for the taste and feel of her, but strangely enough, the brief kisses they'd shared had only made his hunger worse. Before, he'd only had his imaginings; now, he knew ex-actly what it felt like to have her in his arms and he wanted more. Lots more.

Conal totally lost his train of thought as Livvy bent over to close her suitcase and the well-worn jeans tightened over her hips. His eyes narrowed as he savored the sight. She had the most fantastic shape, slim and yet femininely rounded. The only way she could look any better would be if she were naked. He gulped as he felt sweat pop out on his forehead.

You're in a bad way, Sutherland, he told himself. *You need a woman.* No, he corrected himself. He didn't need a woman; he needed Livvy Farrell and he needed her very badly. He was getting damn sick and tired of spending hours every evening trying to work off his frustrations in the gym.

The snick of Livvy's suitcase locking echoed loudly in the still apartment, cutting through his thoughts.

"Is that all you're taking?" He gestured toward the case.

"That and five dozen bagels."

Conal blinked. "Five dozen bagels?" he repeated. "What are you going to do with five dozen bagels?"

Livvy grinned at him. "At the risk of appearing obvious, I'm going to eat them. Or rather, my mother is going to serve them at the buffet dinner this evening. Mom swears that only a real New Yorker can make a proper bagel."

"She's right. You get the bagels, and I'll bring the suitcase."

Livvy grabbed the bagel sack off her kitchen counter, checked once more to make sure that everything was turned off and hurried after Conal who was carrying her heavy suitcase as if it weighted no more than a few pounds.

She stole a furtive glance at his upper arm. Just how strong was he? she wondered. He'd played professional football until two years ago when he'd retired and opened the ad agency. Football players were supposed to be very strong.

Maybe she would have a chance to explore the exact state of his musculature over the weekend. A shiver of anticipation danced over her skin. The possibilities seemed endless.

To Livvy's surprise, Conal was a competent driver who showed an amazing patience for the idiosyncrasies of the other drivers on the road. Apparently he had escaped the macho speed syndrome that had infected so many of the men she'd dated over the years.

"Now where?" Conal asked her, once they had left the expressway in Scranton.

"Turn right at the light and go straight for a while."

"Interesting place." Conal glanced curiously at the old houses that lined the hilly streets. "Did you grow up here?"

"Uh-huh. My family has been in the Scranton area for a hundred and fifty years. Before that, they starved in Ireland.

"Turn right at the next light," she said absently, as she tried to decide what she should tell him about her family. Should she warn him about potential conversation pitfalls like mentioning the health hazards of smoking to her great-uncle Harry, or politics to her aunt Rose, or tax audits to her grandfather, or the state of the public school system to her cousin Henry? It seemed kind of unfair to let Conal meet her family with the assumption that they were all rational adults who would respond to seemingly innocuous conversational gambits politely.

Livvy shifted in the rental car's soft leather seat, feeling guilty at what she was letting Conal in for. He probably came from a nice, normal family whose members were all polite to guests no matter what the provocation. Not that she knew much about his family background. In fact... Livvy frowned as she searched her memory, she knew almost nothing about Conal's background, period. Just that he'd played pro football and worked in the advertising business in the off-season until an injury to his knee had forced his retirement. That and the fact that he'd wanted to belong to a big family when he'd been a kid.

Her feeling of unease grew the more she thought about it. Why hadn't Conal ever mentioned his family to her? Because he didn't believe in mixing his work life with his personal life, and he didn't foresee her, or really *any* woman, ever occupying a meaningful niche in his personal life? Strangely enough, the thought made her feel slightly more optimistic. Conal had absolutely no idea that she harbored long-range plans where he was concerned. No idea that she wanted a whole lot more than just a weekend from him. And since he didn't know he wouldn't be on guard. If she were lucky, she might be able to slip underneath his defenses before he realized what had happened. If she were very lucky, she might also find out why he seemed to have ruled out a wife and children for himself.

She glanced sideways at Conal, her eyes lingering on the strong line of his square-cut jaw. Slipping under Conal would be a distinct pleasure. Livvy shifted restlessly as the memory of his lips pressing against hers sent a burning sensation over her nerve endings.

Even though she didn't begin to understand it, kissing Conal was far more than she'd ever believed a simple kiss could be. Far more than her previous experiences would have led her to believe was possible. Which made her wonder what making love to him would be like. Her breathing developed an uneven cadence.

"Turn left at the next corner." Livvy gamely tried to redirect her thoughts toward something harmless. "My mother lives at the top of the hill in the yellow house on the right. The one with the car with the Maryland license plates on it, parked in front," she added slowly. Had her uncle David and his family come, after all?

Conal shot her a quick glance as he deftly parked. "What's the matter?"

"Matter? Why should anything be the matter?"

"I asked first. Tell me—after driving all this way, are we just going to sit in the car? I promise not to do anything too unsociable."

The note of uncertainty she heard in his voice surprised her. Could Conal be nervous? He always seemed to be so in control of himself and the situations he found himself in. That he might have a few insecurities himself had never occurred to her before. And she wished it hadn't now, she admitted. She had enough to worry about without worrying about Conal, too.

"I don't know whether you consider it a plus or a minus, but in my family, not doing anything unsociable would probably make you unique," Livvy said.

To her shock, Conal responded by suddenly grabbing her and tugging her across the car seat toward him. She landed awkwardly, her breasts squashing into his chest. A torrent of sensation slammed through her, bringing her emotions clamoring to life.

"What are you doing?" Livvy mumbled, knowing the question was ridiculous, but using it to gain some time to deal with the feelings he so effortlessly raised in her.

"Getting into the role of a besottedly engaged man," he told her. "And what better way than to kiss the object of my affections."

Livvy stared into his eyes. He had such gorgeous eyes, she thought distractedly. Dark and velvety with thick brown lashes. She felt as if she could drown in them. As if— Her thoughts scattered as he leaned closer, and his lips captured hers.

They were warm and firm, and they pressed insistently against hers. Livvy shivered violently as his tongue traced over her full lips, and she mindlessly opened her mouth welcoming his deepening of their kiss. His tongue moved over hers and a tiny moan bubbled out of her throat to be swallowed up by Conal.

"I'm beginning to feel engaged," he muttered against her tingling lips. "But not quite.

"Unfortunately for my mood enhancement, someone is staring at us from the house next door," he added.

Livvy turned her head, following Conal's glance. There was a scruffy-looking young man peering at them, a peeved expression on his face. The neighbor's husband's second cousin's son? If so, she was doubly grateful not to have to dodge him all weekend.

"My rival?" Conal casually leaned over and brushed his lips across her cheekbone. Livvy's reaction was not so casual. Heat from his lips seeped into her skin, warming it and making her wish they were anywhere but in a car in plain sight of anyone who cared to look. But then, the only reason he was kissing her was precisely because they were in plain sight of everyone, she reminded herself.

Determinedly she scooted away from Conal and reached for the door handle. "Let's go inside before Mom comes out and we have the whole street watching the introductions."

Livvy climbed out of the car and waited for Conal to reach her before she started up the front walk. She let out a squeak and spun around when she felt a gentle pinch on her rear.

"Conal Sutherland!"

Conal gave her an impossibly innocent look. "Engaged couples don't do that?"

"This engaged couple doesn't do that."

"That's not quite accurate, since I just did," he said. "Perhaps you should say that your half of this engaged couple doesn't do that."

"Darling, come in. I've been waiting all afternoon for you." Marie's welcoming voice called to Livvy from the open door.

Livvy glanced over her shoulder and hissed at Conal, "Behave yourself," as she hurried through the front door, giving her mother a warm hug.

"Darling, you look wonderful and this must be..." Marie stared past her at Conal.

"Mom, I'd like you to meet Conal Sutherland. He's—"

"Darling!" Marie shrieked as she caught sight of the engagement ring Livvy was wearing. "You said yes!"

Livvy winced at the ecstatic note in her mother's voice.

"I'm so pleased to meet you, Conal. You can call me Marie." She dimpled happily at him. "That's what my other son-in-law calls me."

"Marie," Conal obediently repeated.

A high-pitched shriek followed by a thud echoed down the stairwell from the second floor, and Marie glanced nervously at the ceiling as the chandelier swayed. "Oh, dear," she murmured.

Livvy blinked as a second thud followed the first.

"It doesn't sound as if they're taking prisoners up there," Conal offered.

Livvy jumped as yet a still-louder thump sounded. "Um, Mom, do you think we ought to see what happened?"

Marie vigorously shook her head. "I'm quite sure I don't want to know. It's your cousin Mark. Your uncle David sent him upstairs and told him to stay there until he decided to behave."

"They won't be here that long," Livvy muttered. "I thought Uncle David said they couldn't come?"

"He did!" Marie whispered confidentially. "They simply appeared an hour ago saying that they found they were able to make it after all. And I can't find anyplace for them to stay. I've called every single one of our relatives, and they all said they haven't got one spare bed."

Livvy grimaced. "Do you blame them? Those kids of theirs are completely out of control. Why don't you send them to a hotel?"

Marie looked shocked. "Darling, I can't do that. They're family. I love David and Sarah."

"I love them, too, but I've found my feelings for them increase the farther I am from their kids."

"Shh," Marie muttered. "They'll hear you. Come on."

"Fascinating," Conal murmured as they followed Marie into the living room. Livvy wondered whether he was referring to the continuing noise from upstairs or her mother. Either one was probably outside his experience.

"Welcome to the family!" Her uncle David cheerfully wrung Conal's hand. "I don't have to tell you you're getting a girl in a million with Livvy."

"We're so glad to meet you, Conal," Sarah gushed. "My daughters will be so excited. You will let them be your bridesmaids won't you, Livvy?"

"Um, I haven't gotten to the planning stage yet," Livvy stalled.

"Take my advice, Conal, and elope," David said.

"Livvy, darling," Marie said, "would you help me a minute in the kitchen?"

"Come on, Conal," Livvy said, unwilling to leave him alone with her relatives. David would probably launch into one of his incredibly boring fishing stories.

"Darling, I hate to ask this of you," Marie said the minute the kitchen door was safely closed behind them, "but I can't think of what else to do. Would you and Conal mind dreadfully spending the weekend at your sister's? Fern flatly refused to take any of David's kids. She said she still hasn't gotten the grape-juice stains out of her carpet from the last time they were there." Marie shook her head. "And Fern a teacher, too. You'd think she could know how to handle them."

"With a whip and chair," Livvy muttered, but her mother ignored her.

"But she said she'd love to have you and Conal," Marie said.

"We would be happy to stay at Fern's," Conal promptly said, and Marie gave him a grateful smile.

"You're so kind," Marie said.

Kind? Livvy examined her mother's description and found that it was true. Conal was kind. Not the cloying, patronizing variety of *kind,* but the bracing, practical type.

"You'll just have time to get over to Fern's and unpack before it's time to go to Olivia's for dinner. And for heaven's sake don't be late," Marie warned. "Olivia is already mad that Mom and Dad won't be there tonight. She seems to think that it's my fault that Dad's doctor said he had to rest tonight if he was going to have the whole family out to the farm tomorrow. And make sure you take the bagels with you. You did remember them, didn't you?"

At Livvy's nod, Marie stood on tiptoe and gave Conal a kiss on his cheek before she enveloped Livvy in a hug. "I can hardly wait to show off my soon-to-be son-in-law. I hope you aren't going to have a long engagement, dear?"

"It couldn't be too short as far as I'm concerned," Conal said, and Livvy winced at the laughter she could hear coloring his voice. As usual her mother was oblivious to nuances.

"Wonderful!" Marie clapped her hands together in pleasure. "I've always loved Christmas weddings."

"Or Thanksgiving," Conal added.

Livvy gave him a quelling glare as she dragged him toward the back door. Playing a part was one thing, hamming it up quite another.

Three

"There, that's Fern's place." Livvy pointed to a small yellow cottage with blue shutters wedged in between two much bigger houses. "Her new color combination looks nice," she added.

Conal pulled up in front of Fern's house, cut the engine and took a good look at it. It didn't look nice, he mentally corrected Livvy's assessment. It looked fantastic. Like the stuff dreams were made of. His to be precise. As a child he'd dreamed about living in a house very much like Fern's. One with shutters on the windows, dormers on the second floor and a wide porch across the front with a swing on it. Most of the other kids in the home had fantasized about suddenly discovering that they belonged to parents who were sports heros or movie stars who took them away to live in a mansion. But he never had. His dreams had been much more prosaic. He'd just wanted a father and a mother and a small house where he could sit on the porch on rainy summer afternoons and play.

Conal's eyes drifted to Livvy. Livvy would fit right into a house like that. In the master bedroom. He felt anticipation spiral through him, nibbling at his composure. A master bedroom with a king-size bed, and he would spend his long, rainy afternoons playing in it with Livvy. He would take her in his arms and smother her lovely face with kisses and then he would work his way downward, over her elegant neck to the enticing hollow at the base of her throat. The skin on his body prickled as he anticipated the pleasure of slowly, leisurely undressing her to reveal her delectable body.

He grabbed his imagination by the throat and throttled it, when he realized that his fingers were trembling with the force of his desire. Think of this as an ad campaign, he encouraged himself. You're trying to sell a product, yourself. You have to convince Livvy that you would make the most perfect lover she could ever hope to find.

He stifled a sigh. The problem with that was that he didn't know what characteristics she wanted in a lover. And he wasn't sure how to find out without asking, and that was far too dangerous. Once he'd verbalized his desire for her, the words could never be recalled. They would hang between them. They could well poison their present relationship, which, while emotionally frustrating at times, was a whole lot better than nothing. And that was what he would have if she were to leave. As talented as she was, she could get a job at any one of a dozen advertising agencies tomorrow.

Uncertainly Livvy studied Conal's set expression out of the corner of her eye, wondering what he was thinking about. Certainly not the effectiveness of her sister's color scheme. Was he trying to figure out how to escape back to New York? Had her mother's embarrassing eagerness to welcome him to the family scared him off? Probably not. She relaxed ever so slightly as she studied the determined jut of his chin. It would take far more than her mother to scare Conal Sutherland.

Besides, even if Conal was having second thoughts, they had a deal, she reminded herself. Conal would honor it. And he would get fair value for his impersonation. She was going to do his soup campaign. She shivered as her eyes strayed to his firm lips, like a magnet that was perpetually drawn to true north. She longed to feel them against hers again. She wanted...

Livvy blinked as his face came closer, filling her line of vision. It was as if her intense longing had actually pulled him to her. Nervously she licked her lower lip, afraid to say anything for fear of disturbing whatever he intended to do. Her breath caught in her throat as he came closer. Close enough to brush his lips gently over hers. A tingling sensation shot through her.

Conal felt so good, and he tasted even better, she thought dreamily. She wanted more, much more. She wanted to grab his head and hold him still while she pressed her tongue against his lips. She wanted to run her fingers through his hair and find out if it was as silky as it looked.

She was jolted back to reality with a thump when Conal raised his head and whispered, "There, that should be enough to convince anyone watching that we're an engaged couple."

No, it wasn't, Livvy wanted to say. It takes much more than that. She sighed longingly.

"Tired?" Conal asked.

"A little." Livvy grabbed the excuse he offered. After

getting out of the car, she started toward the house. The door immediately opened to reveal her sister.

"Livvy! I've been waiting all afternoon for you to show up. Is this your Conal? He looks fantastic!" Fern rushed on without waiting for an answer. "If he's half as nice as he is gorgeous, he was well worth waiting for."

"Thank you, but I was the one who had to wait until Livvy made up her mind. But now that she's said yes, I intend to hold on to her." Conal's voice deepened, and even though Livvy knew it was all show for Fern's benefit, she still couldn't suppress the confusing mix of anticipation, pride and desire that churned through her.

Fern's russet eyebrows shot up, and she nodded approvingly. "Romantic, too. Better and better.

"Welcome to the family, Conal." Fern threw her arms around him and gave him a hug.

Livvy tensed at the sight of Fern clinging to Conal's broad chest. She wasn't jealous, Livvy assured herself. Jealousy was the sign of an immature person. And she wasn't immature, even if she did feel a little unsettled at the moment.

"Come on in, you two. I'm glad to have you stay here. Mom tried to get me to take some of Uncle David's kids, but I told her I didn't care if they drummed me out of the family, I wasn't having them again. I tell you Aunt Sarah is ruining them with her idiotic notions about discipline having to come from within instead of being imposed from without. After fourteen years in the classroom, I know perfectly well that children need some limits put on them."

"I really like the new paint job on your house," Livvy said trying to change the subject, not wanting to talk about the down side of raising kids. Her goal this weekend was to convince Conal that marriage and a family were great ideas, not that he'd been right all along to avoid marriage like the plague.

As usual, Fern was not to be sidetracked. Nor did she have any illusions about what Livvy was trying to do. She shot a quick glance at Conal and shrugged. "He has to find out about the skeletons in the family closet some time. It might as well be now."

Livvy grimaced. "This advice from a charter member of the never-do-today-what-you-can-put-off-till-tomorrow club?"

"What a disgusting little sister you turned out to be, and to think you had such promise when you were young," Fern teased.

Conal listened to their good-natured bickering with a faint feeling of nostalgia. His entire childhood had been composed of one gigantic longing to belong to a family. A family who remembered the same things you did and shared your likes and dislikes. A family whose acceptance of you was unconditional. But that kind of longing was for children, he reminded himself, and he was an adult now. Now he could control his own destiny. He didn't need a family for that. And as for shared memories, you didn't have to be related to someone to share memories with them. Maybe if he was lucky, he could build a few memories with Livvy for the future. All he had to do was somehow convince her that they were meant to be lovers.

And he was making progress. He'd actually gotten to kiss Livvy. Several times in fact. Not only that, but he had the whole weekend in front of him. Anything might happen.

Conal followed Fern and Livvy into the house, looking around the comfortable living room curiously. It looked homey and welcoming. Rather like Fern herself.

"It's a good thing the pair of you are engaged," Fern

said, "because otherwise Conal would have had to sleep on the couch, and it has lumps. As it is, I put Bobby in with us on the roll-away bed and you can have his room. Fortunately I haven't gotten around to replacing that old double bed he sleeps on."

Livvy gulped as Fern's words reverberated through her head, churning her emotions into a confused muddle as they went. She felt hot and excited and breathless. And scared, she admitted. She hadn't foreseen them being forced into the immediate intimacy of sharing a room, let alone sharing a bed, when she'd had her bright idea. She'd thought they'd be staying with her mother whose views on sex would have made the Puritans look like a bunch of wild-eyed liberals.

Livvy stole a quick peek at Conal, but it was impossible to tell what he was thinking. His face was impassive, although there was a tiny muscle twitching beside his mouth. Why? Annoyance at being manipulated into this situation? Did he believe she was behind it? Did he think she was trying to manipulate him? Embarrassment slithered through her, tightening her skin. She wanted to assure him that it certainly wasn't her idea. But she couldn't do that. At least, not now. If she said anything, Fern would begin to wonder what was going on, and it wouldn't be long before she found out. And once she did, everyone would know. Fern couldn't keep a secret to save her soul.

"Is that going to be a problem?" Fern asked uncertainly at their continued silence. "I mean, I haven't put my foot in it, have I? You two aren't sexually dysfunctional, are you?"

"No!" Livvy sputtered.

To Livvy's surprise, Conal put his arm around her and pulled her tense body up against his. His large frame seemed to provide a bulwark against Fern's curiosity. It didn't make any sense, but it was true all the same.

"Livvy simply isn't used to our being engaged yet," Conal's deep voice slipped seductively over her nerve endings, and Livvy instinctively pressed closer to his side.

"I forgot! Let me see your ring. Mom called me the minute you left and said it was a beaut."

Livvy obediently held out her hand, torn between a sudden surge of shame at lying and pride at having Conal's taste in rings admired. Pride won.

"Wow!" Fern beamed at Conal. "Much, much better than Mom's next-door neighbor's husband's second cousin's son."

Fern jumped as an alarm went off in the kitchen. "Drat, is it that late already? In case Mom didn't tell you, Aunt Olivia is hosting the family for dinner, and you know what she's like if anyone's late. She's already going to be ticked off at me because Bill has to work late and won't be there until later. Bill's my husband," Fern added, at Conal's confused look.

"How long have we got?" Livvy asked.

"Fifteen minutes, tops. Why don't you unpack while I rescue my contribution to the family dinner from the oven. If you see Bobby, tell him I want him."

"I'll get our suitcases from the car," Conal offered, heading toward the door.

"Your and Livvy's room is the one on the right at the top of the stairs," Fern called after him, before hurrying into the kitchen to turn off the timer.

Livvy slowly made her way upstairs. She felt as if she'd suddenly been dropped onto an emotional roller-coaster that was playing havoc with her normally even temperament. The thought of actually sharing a bed with Conal made her feel giddy with anticipation, but it also made her feel faintly sick with fear. She had been fantasizing about making love to him for so long now that she was afraid of what might happen. Suppose she were to snuggle up to him in her sleep and start to kiss him? Suppose she were to caress him? What would he think if he woke up and found her exploring his body? She winced at the thought. He would probably think she was a sexually frustrated woman with no self-control. And he would be right. At least as far as he was concerned.

"Why you makin' faces, Aunt Livvy?"

Livvy smiled as Fern's son, Bobby, emerged from the bathroom at the end of the hall.

"Hi, Bobby. I was just thinking," she said. "How's school?"

He scowled. "I hate school. When I'm big, I'm never going to go to school again."

"Oh?" Livvy muttered, taken aback. Normally Bobby was full of the wonders of the first grade. "Why?" she finally asked.

"'Cause Mike keeps hitting me, and it hurts," he blurted out, and then glanced fearfully around as if he expected retribution of his complaint.

"Tell the teacher," Livvy suggested.

Bobby gave her a scornful look. "I did, and she said she'd talk to him, but it didn't do no good. He hits me when she can't see."

"Bullies rarely respond to reason," Conal said from the bottom of the stairs.

Livvy swung around and peered down at him. The sun coming in through the stained-glass window above the stairwell bathed his hair in colored lights, reminding Livvy of a Christmas tree. Her own private Christmas tree. Or better yet, her Christmas present. Tied up in a red bow. Her eyelids began to feel heavy as she imagined him wearing a wide red bow and nothing else. Where should she put it? she wondered. Across his broad chest? Or maybe lower. Draped around his abdomen with the bow almost obscuring—

"Who's he?" Bobby's hissed question interrupted Livvy's delightful thoughts.

She blinked and mentally scrambled for a semblance of normalcy, something that was becoming harder and harder to maintain around Conal. "That's my friend, Conal Sutherland."

Bobby stared at Conal. "He's big, ain't he? Mike wouldn't dare hit me if I was as big as him."

"Try hitting Mike back," Conal suggested.

"Mom says that fighting is unacceptable," Bobby said mournfully.

"That reminds me. Your mother wants you, Bobby," Livvy said.

Bobby hunched his shoulders disinterestedly, although he did start down the stairs. He paused at the bottom and shouted back up, "Just you remember that you and him gotta go home on Sunday, Aunt Livvy, cause I don't like to share with Mom and Dad. He snores."

"This is my world and welcome to it," Livvy muttered. Somehow she hadn't quite realized just how uninhibited her family was until she'd been forced to see them through Conal's eyes. What did he think about them? Really? Were they radically different from his own family? Probably, she conceded. Judging from Conal's manners and his outlook on life, he undoubtedly came from a family of highly educated, very proper professionals.

Pushing open the bedroom door, she stared at the double bed, which dominated the small room. The hair on the back of her neck prickled, and she tensed as she felt Conal crowd into the room behind her. She wanted to share that bed with him so much, and yet perversely, she was pet-rified that she would blow her chance and never get an-other one.

"You don't have to look so worried," Conal snapped. "I'm not so hard up for a woman that I've taken to at-tacking them." He set their suitcases down with a thump.

Livvy reacted instinctively to the pain she could hear underlying his words. Pain that she had inadvertently caused. She couldn't bear the thought of Conal suffering at her hands, even the embarrassing truth was better than that.

"I'm not worried about what you might do," she said honestly. "I'm worried about what you might think."

Conal frowned at her. "What are you talking about?"

"I was afraid that you might think I'd engineered this," she said as she waved her hand around the room. "I'm perfectly aware that you're far too attractive to have to resort to manhandling women."

Conal felt his nervous tension ease slightly at her words. Did she really think he was attractive or was she just saying that to make him feel better? He stared into her bright blue eyes, trying to read the emotions he could see shimmering beneath their surface. It was hopeless. He felt as if he were drowning in their depths. He wanted to take her in his arms and squeeze her up against him. He wanted to feel her naked breasts pressing against his bare chest. He wanted to cover every square inch of her ex-quisite skin with kisses. And he wanted to watch her eyes while he did it. He wanted to see if the blue in them deepened.

"Really," Livvy added uncertainly when he simply continued to stare at her.

"Why?" he finally asked, in the hope that if he got her

thinking about attraction and sex it might eventually lead to the real thing.

Livvy frowned. "Why what?"

"Why do you think I'm attractive?"

Livvy opened her mouth and then closed it when nothing came out. What could she say? I'm obsessed with the thought of you. With your looks. With your sharp intelligence and your dry sense of humor. With the fascinating little quirks in your personality. So much so that I spend hours every weekend painting pictures of you in suggestive poses to try to satisfy my craving for you and it's never enough. Never even vaguely enough. She couldn't be that honest. Not only would an admission of her one-sided love be acutely embarrassing, but it made her sound so...juvenile. Like an adolescent in the throes of a giant crush.

But what if she admitted to finding him attractive, without letting him see the depth of her fascination? What if Conal thought that she simply found him attractive and liked kissing him, but didn't attach any special significance to it?

Longing swelled in her throat, threatening to choke her. She wasn't sure what the results would be. All she knew was that she had to try. If she didn't, she would regret it for the rest of her life.

"I'm not precisely sure what I find most attractive about you," she said slowly.

"Oh? How about my muscles?" he asked.

Livvy cautiously watched the deepening twinkle in his eyes. "I hadn't really thought much about your physical appearance," she lied.

"Well, you should," he said in seeming seriousness. "Physical appearance is very important in a relationship, even a pretend one. Why don't you touch me so that you can properly appreciate my physical makeup.''

Livvy blinked. If she had a much greater appreciation of his physical makeup, she would be in danger of idolatry!

Slowly, savoring the moment, she inched closer to him until his knit sweater filled her entire line of vision. He certainly did have muscles, she thought appreciatively. He had muscles in places most men didn't even have places. Tentatively she reached out and pushed against his chest. It felt fantastic. Solid, enduring and warm. Much like his personality, she realized. Conal himself was a very solid, enduring kind of man. He wasn't given to sudden enthusiasms that he just as suddenly abandoned. He was the kind of man a woman could count on for the long haul. The kind of man who wouldn't cut and run at the first sign of trouble.

Not that it was likely to do her much good unless she could somehow manage to convince Conal to forgo his aversion to marriage and make a commitment to her. She frowned as she remembered that he'd apparently been willing to make a commitment to the blonde he'd bought her engagement ring for.

''You have a complaint about the way I'm built?'' Conal asked.

Not this side of fantasyland, she thought, making a valiant effort to forget the past and concentrate on the present. Or better yet, the future.

''Maybe you aren't the type of woman who sets much store by mere strength,'' he mused.

Livvy blinked, trying to decide what to say. Admitting that she found the idea of his superior physical strength a turn-on somehow seemed shallow. But shallow or not, she did. Okay, so she was shallow, she thought. Nobody was perfect.

"Maybe you're the type of woman who appreciates a man for his mind?" Conal grinned at her, and his mischievous expression fueled Livvy's excitement.

"Have you considered that I might like the silent type?" she asked.

Conal tilted his head to one side and studied her for a long moment. Suddenly reaching out, he grabbed her arm and tugged her toward him. Caught off guard, Livvy stumbled against his chest, her breath catching at the intoxicating feel of his hard warmth. Deliberately she relaxed against him, letting her body shape itself to his contours. She could feel a slow throbbing begin to pound in her abdomen.

She looked up into his gleaming eyes and muttered, "Why did you do that?"

"Make up your mind, woman! Do you want the gabby type or the strong, silent type?"

Livvy took a deep breath, and the faint fragrance of his cologne trickled into her nostrils. He smelled ever so faintly of lime. She loved the scent of lime. In fact, she loved everything to do with limes. Lime taffy, limeade, lime pie, lime men....

Did Conal taste like lime, too? She nuzzled her face against his neck, smiling slightly when she felt the muscles in his chest tense. Feeling greatly daring, her tongue darted out to taste his skin. His arms tightened convulsively around her body, binding her tightly against him from chest to thigh. Livvy wiggled pleasurably as she felt his hardness pressing up against her. Considering how fascinated she was with him, it seemed only fair that he should respond to her.

"Livvy..." Conal's voice echoed hoarsely in her ears

as she kissed his neck again. He didn't taste of lime, she decided. He tasted of salt and something far more elusive. Something that reached down deep into the essence of her femininity. It made her want to yank him down on the bed, rip off his clothes and make mad, passionate love to him.

She pushed her hands between them and ran them up over his chest, relishing the solid feel of him. Conal Sutherland was the epitome of her masculine ideal. The embodiment of every single one of her erotic fantasies.

Inching her hands up over his shoulders, she locked her fingers around his neck, tugging slightly. She needed to feel his lips against hers. Needed it badly enough to risk a rebuff.

But a rebuff seemed to be the last thing on his mind. Mesmerized, Livvy watched as his lips came closer and closer, and her excitement grew, becoming a roaring caldron of need ringing in her ears. But to her frustration he suddenly tensed and turned his head.

"What is it?" Her voice sounded slurred to her ears.

Conal nodded toward the door, and Livvy blinked, suddenly aware of the fact that her nephew was calling her name. Embarrassment sent a wave of color over her cheeks as she realized just how deeply enthralled she'd been with Conal. She peered up at his face. He didn't look devastated by their interruption. He just looked annoyed. Much like he did when something went wrong in the office.

A chill of reality slithered down her spine, and she hastily stepped back. There was no reason why he should have been so engrossed, she told herself. She was the one with the fixation, not him. He probably enjoyed kissing her as much as any normal man enjoyed kissing a willing woman. She found the thought inordinately depressing.

"Aunt Livvy." Bobby's impatient voice bludgeoned her incipient self-pity. "Why don't you answer me? What are you doing in there? I have to get some clean socks outa my drawer."

"We're—" Conal began, but Livvy hastily interrupted him, afraid he might be one of those adults who believed in telling children the plain, unvarnished truth.

"Just unpacking, Bobby." Livvy tried her best to sound normal. "You can come in if you like."

"Can we vote on it?" Conal whispered, and Livvy immediately felt better. Conal did mind being interrupted.

Bobby shoved open the door and rushed over to his dresser. "Mom told me to get changed, but she also told me that I wasn't to go in if you had the door closed or I might see more than I should."

He rummaged though his socks, managing to scatter half a dozen pairs on the floor. "But when I asked her what that meant, she just laughed and said I was too young."

"And so you are," Livvy ducked the question even though intellectually she thought that it deserved an honest answer. Just not by her. She didn't understand what was going on between her and Conal any too well herself. Certainly not well enough to put it in terms a six-year-old could understand.

"We'd better go downstairs," Livvy forced herself to say, when what she really wanted to do was to wait until Bobby had left and then go back to kissing Conal. But there was no guarantee that Bobby would leave the room. Not while he thought he might be missing something. And not only that, but she didn't want Conal to think she was immediately angling for another kiss, even if it was true. She would just have to figure out a way to get back in his arms that appeared accidental.

Livvy squinted thoughtfully as she left the bedroom with Conal right behind her and Bobby bringing up the rear. Maybe she could use that time-honored cliché about pretending to trip and let him catch her?

No. Regretfully she rejected the idea. She had to be behind him for that ploy to have any hope of success and she was already in front. Maybe—

She squeaked in sudden fright and frantically grabbed for the banister as her foot stepped on something that moved. Not only moved but also let out an ear-piercing howl and took a vicious swipe at her leg before exploding downstairs in a burst of outraged black fur.

"What the hell was that?" Conal grabbed her, steadying her trembling body against his.

"Mind the cat, Livvy," Fern yelled from the kitchen. "I forgot to tell you, he's taken up sleeping on the stairs."

"That's not a cat. That's a disaster." Conal's large hand rubbed comfortingly across the taut muscles of Livvy's back. She could feel them loosening, warming to his ministration.

"True," she murmured against his chest, wondering how long she could pretend to be shaken. "But I can't complain."

"I can." His hand moved a little higher, kneading the muscles in her shoulders.

Livvy allowed herself to sag against him. "I meant I shouldn't complain. I found that monster abandoned by the side of the road last year and poor old Fern agreed to give it a home."

"Better she should have agreed to teach it some manners," Conal's breath wafted enticingly over her cheek.

"Hmm," Livvy murmured, afraid to move a muscle for fear of distracting him from what she hoped he was going to do—kiss her. She must remember to buy the cat a new toy, she thought foggily a second before Conal's lips met hers and she ceased thinking at all and merely felt. Felt his hardness and the heat of his lips. Shivers chased over her as his hand speared through her hair, holding her head steady as he exerted pressure on her mouth.

Eagerly she parted her lips as Conal's tongue traced hotly over her bottom lip. She could feel herself sinking into a whirlpool of sexual need that was bottomless. It seemed unbelievable that simply kissing someone could make her feel like this. Like she could fly off into a golden tomorrow and never have to face the harsh realities of life again.

Conal's arms tightened instinctively as he felt her tremble in his grasp. He couldn't believe how good kissing her felt. It made him almost afraid to contemplate what might happen if he were lucky enough to make love to her. He would probably explode from the sheer pleasure of it. But what a way to go.

A prickly sensation that had nothing to do with Livvy pierced his sense of euphoria. He tried to ignore the unsettling feeling, but it refused to go away. He slowly raised his head to find himself staring into a huge blue eye inches from his own.

Bobby! The sight was more effective than a cold shower on his overheated emotions.

"What ya doin' with my aunt Livvy, mister?" Bobby demanded.

Conal reluctantly let go of Livvy when he felt her tense in his arms.

"Didn't your mother ever tell you not to ask personal questions?" Conal countered, not sure what he should say. The only thing he was sure of at the moment was that he wished the kid were elsewhere. Anywhere but where he was.

"No," Bobby said. "Why was you kissin' Aunt Livvy like that?"

"Never mind what your aunt and I were doing," Conal said, embarrassment making his voice curt. Were all kids as intrusive as this one seemed to be? he wondered uncertainly. His experience with children was limited to making admiring sounds when his friends regaled him with improbable stories of their offsprings' latest achievements. At the home where he'd been raised, the children had been segregated by age and he hadn't had anything to do with the younger ones. If all kids were like Bobby... Conal barely repressed a shudder, glad for once of the fact that he wasn't going to have children of his own. The thought of his own child eyeing him with Bobby's icy look of disdain chilled his soul.

"Bobby, put your socks on. We're leaving in five minutes," Fern ordered from the foot of the stairs.

She waited until Bobby had scampered back upstairs and then turned to Conal. "Sorry about that. He's a little precocious."

Conal tried to keep his face expressionless. Even though he wanted to tell Fern that if her son didn't stop interfering with his attempts to kiss Livvy, he was going to discover the error of his ways.

"Umm, why don't you wait for us in the living room, Conal?" Fern said. "Livvy, would you unmold my gelatin salad? I always manage to break it."

"Sure, Fern." Livvy regretfully followed her sister into the kitchen. She didn't want to unmold a salad; she wanted to go back to kissing Conal.

"It's too bad your Conal doesn't like kids," Fern said as she handed Livvy the bright red salad mold.

"He does, too," Livvy automatically defended him, having no idea if it was true or not. She just couldn't believe that a man as nice as Conal was wouldn't like children.

"He sure didn't seem to like poor little Bobby," Fern insisted. "He was frowning at him, and when I said something, Conal just stared at me."

"That's because he's too well mannered to tell you what he really thought," Livvy rationalized as she held the mold under the hot tap water.

Livvy deftly unmolded the jellied salad on the plate Fern held out. "You can hardly blame him for being less than enthusiastic about having some strange kid interrupt him in the middle of kissing his fiancée twice within the space of minutes."

"Maybe," Fern said. "I will admit I'd almost forgotten what it's like when you're first engaged. Bill and I couldn't keep our hands off each other. And to think that—" She sighed despondently.

"Is something wrong?"

"No, not a thing," Fern said with a determined brightness that worried Livvy. "Everything's great. I think this is the best second-grade class I've ever had. The kids are absolute darlings. I could never give up teaching!" Her voice hardened.

Livvy blinked at her vehement tone. "There's no reason why you should, is there?" she asked cautiously.

"Some people think teaching jobs grow on trees! Why, do you remember how long I had to do substitute teaching before I got my own classroom? Six years, that's how long."

"Oh?" Livvy muttered, wondering what it was all about. Was the school board thinking of cutting the teaching staff? But surely if that was all it was, Fern would have said so.

"Oh, dear, would you look at that time," Fern said, changing the subject. "You must be eager to get over to Aunt Olivia's and show off that rock. To say nothing of Conal himself."

"I hope I'm not so petty." Livvy tried to look virtuous, but it was a dismal failure. Petty it might be, but she was looking forward to showing off Conal to her relatives, particularly some of the older, more interfering ones. Although, what they might say when the engagement was broken was anybody's guess.

She frowned as she went to find Conal. She didn't really want to set him up as the villain, if things didn't work out as she was praying they would. He didn't deserve to be thought of badly.

Four

"**W**hy are you staring at me as if I'd just grown another head?" Conal demanded.

"I was just thinking," Livvy said. "You wouldn't happen to have a couple of ex-wives hanging around, would you?" She tried to look only marginally interested in the answer, not wanting him to realize just how intensely curious she was about his past.

Conal blinked, taken aback by the unexpected question. "Not even one. You're the first woman I've ever even been engaged to."

Livvy ignored the warm glow that spiraled through her, reminding herself that he wasn't engaged to her, either. He was merely fulfilling an agreement.

"What about a possessive lover or a child or two?" she persisted, determined to find out everything she could while she had the chance.

To her surprise, Conal's face hardened.

"I have not fathered any children, ever!"

"I see," Livvy said weakly, wondering why her question had produced such a violent reaction, but leery of asking. Not only might her sister return any minute and interrupt them, but also Conal did not look in any mood to give her a rational answer.

"Exactly what is it you want to know?" he asked.

Everything, anything, Livvy thought. Where Conal was concerned, her curiosity was insatiable.

"I was thinking about reasons I could give my family when we break off the engagement," she finally said. "I'll have to tell them something. And some of the older members have really ironclad ideas on right and wrong."

"I take it former marriages and illegitimate kids come under the heading of wrongs?"

"Don't say that."

"Say what?"

"Illegitimate kids. As if their parents playing fast and loose with society's rules is somehow the kids' fault."

Conal felt a strange sensation unfurl in his chest at her earnest expression. As if his whole body had been holding its breath and was now free to relax. Illegitimacy wasn't important to Livvy.

"But to get back to our problem, we—" Livvy broke off as Bobby raced down the stairs and into the living room.

"Where's Mom?" he demanded.

"Out in the kitchen getting ready to go," Livvy said.

"I wish I didn't have to go. Great-Aunt Olivia kisses me! I hate it!"

Bobby peered at Conal. "Why don't you kiss Great-Aunt Olivia instead? You liked kissing Aunt Livvy."

"I kiss your Aunt Livvy because I'm engaged to her,"

Conal said. "And I'm not engaged to your great-aunt Olivia."

"I don't see what difference that makes," Bobby grumbled. Plopping down on the sofa, he stared at Conal.

Conal shifted uncomfortably under the child's unwavering stare, searching for something to say to him. What did one say to a six-year-old? None of the polite gambits he normally used with adults would be likely to work.

"Come on, you guys!" Fern yelled from the kitchen. "We have to get a move on."

Conal eagerly got to his feet. He didn't know what Aunt Olivia would be like, but it couldn't be any worse than trying to find something to say to Bobby.

It didn't take Conal five minutes to realize that he might have been too hasty in his judgment. And that he might have wasted a good part of his childhood fantasizing about the joys of belonging to a large family. The reality, at least as it was presented by Livvy's family, was fraught with pitfalls.

His first hint that not all of Livvy's family were disciples of Miss Manners's dictates came before he even made it into Aunt Olivia's house. One of the four elderly men sitting on the porch eyed him through the blue smoke of a evil-smelling cigar and said, "This your intended, Livvy? Big as he is, he'll run to fat later. You mark my words."

"Conal, the tactful one is my great-uncle Shamus. And the rest are my great-uncles Harry, Leo and Isaac. This is Conal Sutherland."

Livvy possessively put her hand on Conal's arm, forgetting at the feel of his muscular strength, what she'd been about to add. Conal felt so good, she thought dreamily. So absolutely wonderful. What would his whole body feel like? His whole naked body? She remembered the double bed waiting for them back at Fern's and a flush burned over her cheekbones. Did Conal wear pajamas to bed? she suddenly wondered. If he didn't, and he hadn't brought anything because he hadn't expected to be sharing his room... Her flush deepened.

"Ha!" Harry cackled. "It must be love the way she's gone off into a trance."

"Why else would one get engaged?" Livvy hedged.

"Lots a reasons!" Leo's eyes dropped to her slender waist, and he suddenly glared at Conal. "You ain't been doing anything you shouldn't with our Livvy, have you?"

Livvy winced.

"Take it easy, Leo," Harry said soothingly. "The boy's marrying Livvy, and as long as he's what she wants, that should be enough."

"He is." Livvy nodded emphatically. "Exactly what I want. Conal is perfect."

Conal was caught by surprise at the instinctive feeling of pride and anticipation that filled him even though he knew that her words were no more than part of the role she was playing. What would it be like if she were to really mean them? If she really did think that he was everything she wanted?

"You smoke, boy, or are you one of *them?*" Isaac demanded.

Conal blinked, struggling to mentally shift gears. Who was them?

"He doesn't smoke," Livvy answered for him.

"Oh, and doesn't he talk, either?" Harry asked.

Shamus shook his head mournfully at Conal. "Been married sixty-one years, son, and I'll give you a piece of advice. Begin as you mean to go on. You let Livvy 'bear lead' you now, and you'll be living under the cat's paw your entire life.''

"I am not 'bear leading' him," Livvy protested. "I'm not even sure what it means.''

"She's a spirited woman, son." Shamus ignored her. "You got to show her who's boss right from the start. And a good place to start would be that job of hers. Now that she's found herself a husband, she should quit. A woman should be home cooking supper and minding the kids, not running around a big city.''

Livvy bit back the urge to say something very rude. She had been arguing with her elderly relations since she was old enough to understand what they were saying, and they hadn't listened to her arguments yet. There was no reason to assume they were going to start now.

"She can't quit." Conal put his arm around Livvy's waist and pulled her up against his side. "I couldn't get along without her at the office.''

The unmistakable sincerity in Conal's voice helped to soothe Livvy's ruffled temper. Her uncles' views didn't really matter. It was Conal's that did. She'd never seen any evidence that he objected to working wives. Just to wives in general. The thought effectively squashed her pleasure.

Isaac snorted. "That's the trouble with the world today. Nobody knows their place.''

"I think my place is helping Mom," Livvy grabbed the excuse to escape. She loved her elderly uncles dearly, but occasionally she wanted to throttle them.

"Sorry about that," she muttered to Conal once they were inside.

"Livvy! Let me see your ring." Livvy's least favorite aunt, May, hurried across the room toward them.

Livvy obediently held out her left hand, trying not to

look smug. For years now, Aunt May had been snidely comparing Livvy's unmarried state to that of her own long-married daughters. Now Livvy not only had a fiancé, but he was gorgeous, well educated, wealthy and just plain nice.

"It almost looks real," May sneered.

"It is real," Conal stated smoothly. "As real as my love for Livvy."

If only it were true, Livvy felt a flash of longing so intense it was painful.

"Really?" May looked uncertainly at Conal. She wasn't used to having the men in the family stand up to her. As a general rule, they tried to avoid her razor-sharp tongue, and when that was impossible, they endured her bad manners in silence in the hope that she would lose interest and go torment someone else.

"If you'll excuse us, Aunt May, I want to find Mom." Livvy tugged Conal toward the kitchen. They were waylaid by Livvy's teenaged cousin, Emily, who looked at Conal as if he were an unexpected gift from heaven and slunk over to them.

Livvy bit back an exasperated sigh at her cousin's exaggerated walk and her attempt at a sexy expression. Emily was basically a good kid who had recently discovered the male gender and was still working on her technique. Livvy just wished she would confine her practice to boys her own age.

"Conal, this is my cousin Emily." Livvy glanced at Conal to find him watching Emily with the same expression he'd worn one afternoon when the two of them had gone to the zoo to get some ideas for an ad campaign for animal crackers. Livvy couldn't decide whether to be amused or annoyed, so she finally opted to ignore it.

"I'm so glad to meet you, Conal," Emily breathed

soulfully, and batted her heavily mascaraed eyelashes at him.

"And I, you." Conal watched the dried flecks of the mascara fly off Emily's lashes.

"We'll see you later, Emily," Livvy said as she pulled Conal into the dinning room.

"How old is that kid?" Conal asked. He glanced over his shoulder to see Emily gazing after him with a look that reminded him of a hungry dog he'd once fed.

"Thirteen," Livvy said. "Don't worry. It's nothing personal. You're just a good-looking older man, and she wants to try to fascinate you."

Conal chuckled. "I do find her fascinating but not for the reasons that she probably wants. You know, you always seem like such a self-contained person. It's strange to think that all these people are related to you."

Self-contained? Livvy weighed his description. If only he knew how very unself-contained she could be.

"Actually this is only a fraction of them. All of my grandparents came from huge families, and they all married and had big families. It wasn't until my generation that smaller families became a little more common."

Too bad customs had changed, Conal thought. Livvy would be a natural as the matriarch of a large clan. He could easily see her with six or seven children of her own. Sturdy little boys who liked to play football in the fall and baseball in the summer. A shaft of some dark, uncivilized emotion shattered the image. Who would be the man to teach them the rules of the games? The unsettling feeling deepened at the thought of some faceless man taking Livvy in his arms and kissing her. And of his taking her into his bed.

It wasn't any of his business what Livvy chose to do with her life, he thought, trying to neutralize his corrosive feelings. Nor would he care after his desire for her had burned itself out. As it undoubtedly would if he could just make love to her a few times. Anything as intense as his desire for her couldn't last. Afterward, he wouldn't care if she married someone else. If she had kids. In fact, he would be glad, he assured himself. Livvy deserved someone to love her. Someone to marry her and spend his life making her happy.

And he had long ago accepted that he wouldn't marry. That he couldn't marry.

The memory of Eva's sadly sympathetic eyes as she'd refused his long-ago offer of marriage scraped through his memory like sandpaper. He'd met her his senior year of college and she was the first woman he'd ever been serious about. Serious enough to assume that her professions of love meant that she would marry him when he asked. She'd quickly disabused him of that notion. Eva had quoted psychological study after psychological study on the dangers involved in marrying a man who had no first-hand knowledge of how families operated to draw on; and told him that, while she would always cherish the memory of their affair, she simply couldn't risk marrying him.

His first reaction had been disbelief and then anger and finally resignation when he'd read the studies for himself. Read them and a score of others in his attempt to find some mitigating factors. But he hadn't. Not really.

He knew that if he married he would just make a mess of being a husband and wind up with Livvy hating his guts. Pain twisted through him at the thought, and he hastily throttled it.

"You'd think at my age you'd come to me instead of making me come looking for you?" A fragile-looking, old woman leaning on a cane hobbled up to them, distracting Conal from his unhappy thoughts.

"Nona! I didn't know you were here, or I'd have introduced you first thing." Livvy gently hugged the frail woman.

"I was in the study looking at that thing your uncle Paul bought." Nona grimaced. "It is my considered opinion that it is an invention of the devil and should be burned."

Livvy blinked, trying to imagine what her staid uncle Paul could possibly have bought that would come under that heading.

"There were pictures of naked females on it," Nona continued in remembered outrage, "and when I said something, your cousin Sam said that he knew where to find pictures of men and women doing heaven knows what else."

The problem being that Sam knew what they were doing, Livvy suddenly understood.

"She was surfing the internet," Livvy told the confused-looking Conal.

Conal studied the old woman's furious features and decided that his best bet would be to say nothing. People who wanted to censor things didn't want to hear his views on the inviolability of the First Amendment.

"Conal, this is Nona. Grandfather Farrell's mother. She's the family matriarch."

"And don't you forget, my girl," Nona said.

"See my ring, Nona." She tried to head off the catechism she feared was coming. Nona in this mood could be daunting and embarrassingly frank.

"Bah! What's a hunk of compressed coal matter, girl? It's the man who gives it to you that's important."

"Conal is exactly what I want," Livvy tried. "He's perfect."

"No man is perfect," Nona shot back. "Even my dear sainted Virgil had a few faults."

Livvy's mouth fell open at the revelation. It was a standing joke in the family that the longer Great-Grandfather Farrell had been dead, the more perfect he became.

"The thing is, can you live with the faults he's got? Ask yourself that, girl. Marriage isn't like buying a suit from the store that you can return if you find it isn't exactly what you want after you get it home. At least, it shouldn't be." Nona shot a disgruntled look across the room at a cousin who had just filed for divorce from her third husband.

Livvy looked up as the door to the kitchen opened to reveal her mother. Marie took one look at Nona and promptly scurried back into the safety of the kitchen.

Livvy suppressed a sigh. She wasn't likely to get any help from that quarter. Whoever had said that families stuck together had never met hers. They were more than happy to sacrifice one member for their own peace of mind.

"And beliefs, that's another thing," Nona continued. "You Catholic?" she shot the question at Conal.

"Um, no," Conal admitted.

"Not Catholic!" Nona looked appalled. "And you want to marry our Livvy?"

"I'm a Protestant," Conal offered, feeling as if he'd slipped into some weird time warp.

"What denomination?" Nona demanded.

Conal shrugged. "None in particular." In truth, he hadn't been in a church since his boyhood when the orphanage staff had alternated taking them to the Lutheran, Methodist and Presbyterian churches that were within walking distance. There hadn't been any Catholic kids at the home. They had all gone to an institution run by the nuns across town.

"Nona, a man's religion is his own business," Livvy said.

"Not when he wants to marry into my family, it isn't!" Nona's emphatic tone left no room for compromise. "Well, there's no help for it. You're obviously besotted with him. Not that he isn't a handsome broth of a lad," Nona admitted grudgingly. "He'll just have to convert."

"Convert?" Livvy blurted out with a quick glance at Conal. To her relief, he didn't seem angry, he appeared bemused.

"It was good enough for St. Paul, it's good enough for him," Nona nodded decisively. "I'll speak to John about it."

"Lovely," Livvy muttered as Nona hobbled away in search of a fresh victim's life to rearrange.

"Who's John?" Conal asked.

"Her youngest son. He's a Jesuit who worked in South America for decades until he came down with malaria and had to be sent back to the States. He teaches at the University of Scranton now."

Conal shook his head. "I'll say one thing for your family. Things are never dull around them."

Livvy chuckled. "That isn't quite the way I would have put it. Actually, I think the worst is over. Everyone else is either too polite or too vulnerable to try to tell you how to live your life."

"Vulnerable?"

Livvy gave him a wicked smile that sent a shaft of excitement through him. He wanted to absorb the promise of that smile into his very being. And when he'd done that, he wanted to replace it with a smile of sensual contentment. Tonight, he promised himself. Tonight they would be sharing that double bed, and he would have the perfect opportunity to add a hefty dose of reality to their fake engagement.

"They might know my secrets, but I also know theirs," Livvy said. "The rest of the evening should be a snap."

As a prediction it was only partially right. The rest of the people Conal met either seemed to be genuinely glad to see him or else they were totally indifferent to him. But even so he found the evening a strain. It was difficult to remember exactly who all these strange people were. The sheer number of them made him edgy.

Even the arrival of Fern's husband, Bill, who Conal had been expecting to be as friendly as Fern, had been a disappointment. Bill arrived late and clearly had something on his mind. Something unpleasant, judging by his worried, preoccupied manner. Something tied to Fern, Conal finally decided as he watched Bill's eyes constantly stray to her.

Had Bill and Fern reached that point so common in many marriages where the pleasures were drowned out by the day-to-day boredom of everyday living?

Conal's eyes instinctively swung to Livvy who was across the room talking to a very earnest looking young man with a wispy beard. He couldn't imagine ever being bored with Livvy. She brought a sparkle to the most mundane of things.

Joie de vivre the French phrase floated up from his memory. It described Livvy exactly.

Finally, in self-defense, Conal tried to view the evening much as he looked at some of the festivities surrounding the Super Bowl. While he didn't care for the events, his job required him to attend.

"How about some more pie, Conal?" One of the aunts,

whose name he couldn't remember, noticed his empty dessert plate.

"No, thank you," Conal said. "Dinner was delicious, but I couldn't eat another bite." Getting to his feet, he said, "I'll just put my empty plate out in the kitchen. I take it the men are doing the dishes since the women cooked the meal?"

The shocked silence that greeted his words hit him with the force of a blow. He looked around in confusion, his eyes automatically going to Livvy for enlightenment.

She was staring at him with an arrested expression on her face. What had he said? Had he breached some kind of family taboo?

"Downright disheartening, that's what it is," Isaac mourned. "To think that a young man like that should even consider doing woman's work. Ain't natural, I tell you."

"Maybe not, but it's certainly fair," Conal defended himself. He should have known, he thought. He'd been given enough hints of the family's rampant traditionalism.

"Who are you to mettle in the way God has divided labor?" Harry demanded. "You kids always think you know everything."

Conal caught the grin that Livvy quickly hid. It warmed him, making him feel as if the two of them shared a secret that no one else in this crowded room even had an inkling of. Her family might have grave reservations about him, but Livvy didn't. Livvy liked him just the way he was.

The thought sustained him throughout the seemingly interminable evening. Finally, when he was beginning to think that it would never end, it did. With a suddenness that startled him. One minute everyone was talking at the top of their lungs, and the next, they were gathering up their belongings and going.

* * *

"I have the strangest feeling that they all know something I don't," Conal told Livvy as they got into the car.

Livvy chuckled. "Hang around and my great-uncles will tell you in great detail. According to them, they know everything."

Livvy stared out the car window at the flickering lights of Scranton as they sped through its silent streets toward Fern's. A suffocating sense of hope and anticipation and just plain fear churned through her. She wanted so much for this evening to end in Conal's making love to her, but in a strange way she was also afraid that it would happen. Afraid of what it might mean for the future.

Livvy held her breath as Conal pulled up behind her brother-in-law's truck. Maybe it was a mistake to try to figure out what to do, she considered. Maybe she should simply allow events to unfold and see what developed.

Slowly she climbed out of the car and headed toward the well-lit front porch.

"Lock the door behind you, would you?" Fern stuck her head out the kitchen.

Nervously Livvy did as she asked and then turned to Conal. "I guess we should go up," she said.

"Sounds good. I must admit I'm tired."

Tired? Livvy weighed the word as she followed him up the stairs. Tired didn't sound like a man who wanted to kiss her. Was Conal making his excuses in advance? Or was she being paranoid? At the rate she was agonizing over the whole thing, she was likely to pass out from stress and not have to worry.

"You can have first dibs on the bathroom," Livvy said, deciding that that way he would already be in bed by the time she finished. Then, if he wasn't interested in extending their evening, he could pretend to be asleep and that would be an end to the whole thing. At least for tonight.

Livvy plopped down on the bed and watched as Conal extracted his shaving kit, a huge white terry robe and some pajama bottoms from his suitcase. She squinted after him as he left, trying to imagine what he would look like in only that pair of red pajama bottoms. Definitely muscular, the breadth of his chest was easily visible through his shirts, but the texture wasn't. For some reason, every time she painted him, she added a liberal coating of dark hair to his chest. It seemed to suit him.

Livvy pulled her pale yellow nightgown out of her suitcase and eyed it with disfavor. Her nightgowns were bought more for comfort than looks, but even so, she had far sexier ones than this. If she'd had even an inkling that she and Conal wouldn't be staying with her mother... Maybe she could leave some of the tiny buttons on the bodice unbuttoned, she considered. Or would that seem too suggestive? Nervously she bit her lip. She didn't know. She had no idea what Conal might consider provocative sexual behavior.

She gulped as her stomach started to churn. She would play it by ear, she decided, and then shivered as her mind obligingly supplied an image of her with her ear pressed against his naked chest.

No doubt about it, Livvy thought ruefully, she spent far too much time fantasizing about Conal. It had become second nature to her.

She tensed as the door opened to reveal Conal. He looked enormous in the fluffy terry cloth robe he was wearing. Absolutely enormous. Her eyes drifted lower to where the blood red of his pajamas was visible beneath the hem. And lower still to his bare feet.

He had nice feet, she thought distractedly. Big, like the rest of him. Was he that big all over?

"Bathroom's free," Conal's voice sounded husky to her ears.

His words jerked her out of her unsettling thoughts, and she hastily gathered up her nightgown and robe.

"Then I'd better use it before someone else grabs it," Livvy muttered and scooted around him.

Once safely in the bathroom, she leaned back against the closed door and took a deep breath. "You need to put all this into some kind of perspective," she muttered to herself. "What's the worst thing that could happen?"

She would make a fool of herself and Conal would pity her; the thought formed in her mind and she winced. Try focusing on the bright side, she encouraged herself. Fifty years from now she probably wouldn't even remember what had happened tonight.

What would Conal be like in fifty years? Not fat. Livvy rejected her great-uncle's opinion. Conal would probably be on the gaunt side. And his brown hair would undoubtedly be white, but she would bet her last penny his eyes would still sparkle with life and his mind would be every bit as sharp.

"Livvy? Is that you in the bathroom?" Fern's voice interrupted the reverie.

"I'll only be a few minutes." Livvy hurriedly turned on the shower and stepped into its stinging spray.

Five minutes later she was done, although still far from ready to face Conal. Nothing ventured, nothing gained, she told herself.

Livvy hurriedly scampered back to the bedroom before Fern waylaid her. Much as she loved her sister, she most emphatically didn't want to waste time talking to her. Not with Conal lying in her bed.

Livvy inched open the bedroom door and crept inside. Her heart jumped when she saw Conal lying on his back, his hands behind his head. He was staring at her with an intensity that sent a shiver of fear mixed with something else through her.

Now what was she supposed to do? She had made love to him hundreds of times in her imagination, but in her imagination words had never been necessary. He'd always played the part she'd assigned him to perfection. That of besotted lover.

She ran the tip of her tongue over her dry lips. Reality was something else altogether. Now he got to write his own script and who knew what he intended to put in it.

"What's the matter?" Conal's deep voice echoed through her body, vibrating along her bones.

"Nothing." The word escaped on a squeak, and Livvy wanted to groan. So much for the sophisticated approach.

"Then quit hovering there by the door as if you were planning your escape route."

"I already know it. You go out the window onto the porch roof and from there you can jump to the ground." Livvy heard herself rattle off with a feeling of disbelief. She was twenty-nine years old, for heaven's sake. Old enough to be able to hold up her end of the conversation without sounding like a flustered teenager.

"You have something against the door?"

"That's what you should do if there's a fire," she muttered. "One should always know what to do in case of a fire. Fires are very dangerous."

But not half as dangerous as what happens when I open my mouth, Livvy thought wryly.

"Fires may be, but I'm not," Conal said. "Come get into bed."

Trying to appear calm and cool and collected, Livvy started toward the bed only to trip over her shoes, which she'd discarded earlier. With a muffled squeak of dismay, she pitched forward, landing half-on and half-off the bed.

"You're tired." Conal grabbed her upper arms and effortlessly hauled her onto the bed. The feel of his hard fingers biting into her flesh added to her confusion.

"I'm not tired," she muttered, not wanting him to think that she was too tired for anything he might have in mind. Or any idea she might be able to plant in his mind. "I just tripped over my shoes."

Conal chuckled. "I stand corrected. You aren't tired. You're clumsy."

Livvy stifled a sigh of discouragement as she scrambled under the covers. How on earth was she supposed to move the mood from comedy to love? She didn't have the foggiest idea.

Her thoughts fragmented as her foot brushed against his leg. His skin felt hot. Hot and very hard. As if he were nothing but muscle and bone. Didn't her mother used to listen to an old song about a man being nothing but muscles and bone, or was it muscles and blood?

Stop it! Livvy made a superhuman effort to corral her skittering thoughts. She was beginning to feel like a female version of Walter Mitty!

Ask a leading question that can't be answered with a simple yes or no, the advice surfaced from memories of a column on dating she'd once read. She opened her mouth and, to her horror, hiccuped.

No! she thought in anguish. Not hiccups. She hadn't had an attack of nervous hiccups since her junior high school days.

"Do you have the hiccups?" Conal sounded no more than mildly interested.

"No," Livvy insisted and spoiled the denial by another hiccup.

This too will pass. The advice one of her great-aunts was fond of quoting surfaced in her mind, but it brought no comfort whatsoever.

"I know a cure for the hiccups," Conal's voice sounded husky. "It's a form of transference."

"Trans—" Livvy's question was interrupted by another hiccup.

"What you do is distract the sufferer."

Livvy watched as his hand came closer. Her eyes widened as he slowly stroked a finger along her cheekbone and down over her jaw. Sparks seemed to skip from his wandering fingers and into her skin, igniting each and every nerve ending.

Livvy licked her lips as she tried to contain the unexpected feelings rioting through her.

"I—" She hastily closed her mouth on another hiccup.

"Yes?" Conal murmured, and she could feel his warm breath against her cheek. Her soft skin tightened in reaction, and her mouth dried as he leaned closer still. The heat from his large body was pressing against her. Crowding her senses, urging her to snuggle closer to him.

"You're so hot," she muttered, and then winced at his muffled crack of laughter.

"I meant physically, not—" Her voice was swallowed up in a hiccup.

"That's because muscles give off a lot more heat than fat," he murmured, his lips moving from her cheek to her ear. Livvy jumped as he lightly bit her earlobe.

"I am not fat," she muttered, shivering as he began to nuzzle the skin behind her ear. It made her feel so strange. Light-headed, as if she weren't getting enough oxygen and might pass out at any minute.

She took a deep breath to try to counter the effect, and her lungs filled with the scent of him. He smelled so great, she thought distractedly. Like the outside, fresh and clean and crisp and... She gasped as his lips closed over her earlobe and tongued the tender flesh.

"Not fat." His muffled voice against her neck seemed to be directly absorbed into her bloodstream. Like a highly potent stimulus, she thought distractedly. Like she could absorb all of him into her very being and make him a part of her.

"I only meant that women have a layer of fat beneath their skin and men don't," Conal continued as his lips moved slowly down her neck to the hollow at its base.

Livvy trembled as he first kissed the indentation and then lightly licked it. His forehead was brushing her lips, and she was unable to suppress the impulse to kiss him. The slightly salty taste of him flooded her senses, adding to her confusion. Her hand crept up without any conscious thought on her part, and she clutched his shoulders convulsively as his hand brushed over her cotton-covered breasts. She could feel the skin tightening, her nipples convulsing in need. She wanted to yank off her nightgown so she could feel his fingers against her bare flesh.

Livvy twisted slightly, trying to convey her need without resorting to words. Words that she was too uncertain of herself to utter.

"You have the most intriguing distribution of muscle to fat I've ever seen," Conal muttered, but Livvy barely heard the words. She was too busy focusing on the way his breath warmed her skin. She wiggled closer to him, and her leg brushed against the scalding heat of his manhood. She squeezed her eyes shut and inched closer still. He was so overwhelmingly masculine, and she wanted him so very much.

"Livvy, you aren't paying any attention to me." Conal's voice was threaded with laughter. A laughter that wrapped itself around her and raised her spirits, making her feel that anything was possible. As if she were capable of unimagined feats in his arms.

Feeling greatly daring, Livvy reached down and brushed his manhood with her fingers. A surge of triumph hit her as she felt the quiver of reaction that ran through his entire body. She might be highly susceptible to him, but it wasn't a one-way street. He was also susceptible to her. Or could it be that he was just reacting to having a woman in his bed, and it had little to do with her personally? The appalling thought surfaced, but Livvy refused to let it poison her mood. She would worry about why he reacted as he did later. For now it was enough that he did.

"Livvy, I—" His breath escaped on an explosive gasp as her fingers closed around him. Grabbing her hand, he pulled it away from him and placed a hard kiss on her palm. "I'm trying to talk to you, and I can't when you touch me there," he muttered.

"You were right. My hiccups are all gone," she announced, drawing confidence from the deepening tone of his voice. "What's more, I don't have the slightest interest in talking about fat. My own or anyone else's."

"Livvy, I..." She could feel the muscles in his body tensing, and a shiver of uncertainty lanced through her. Was he trying to find a way to tell her that he didn't want to do anything beyond kiss her a little? That while his body might find pleasure in her touch, his mind didn't want it? Livvy could feel her emotions contracting into a tight ball to deflect the anticipated blow of his words.

"I stopped at a drugstore this afternoon before I picked you up..." He paused and Livvy frowned in confusion, not understanding what that had to do with anything.

"To buy condoms." The words erupted from him in a rush.

"Condoms?" Livvy repeated incredulously. Conal had bought condoms before they'd even left New York? He'd wanted to make love to her before he'd even known if he would have the opportunity? Relieved happiness poured through her, making her feel limp.

"Yes." Conal reached under his pillow and picked up the small silver foil packet he placed there. "This condom to be exact.

"I guess what I'm trying to say is that I want to make love to you," he finally blurted out. "But only if you would like to."

Feeling as if she'd somehow managed to slip into one of her fantasies, Livvy gently ran her fingertips over his jawline, relishing the smooth texture of his freshly shaven skin. He felt so fantastic. Maybe that was what she should do, she thought dreamily. Close her eyes and pretend it was all just one of her fantasies.

"Livvy?" Conal captured her hand and held it trapped against his cheek.

"Yes," she said simply. "I would very much like to make love to you."

His arms bound her close, and his lips sought hers with a hungry avidity he made no effort to hide.

Livvy shuddered as her mind struggled to absorb the multitude of sensations bombarding her. She couldn't. They were coming too fast for her to separate each individual one. To savor them as they should be savored. The pressure of his mouth, the touch of his seeking hand as it slipped beneath her nightgown and cupped her breast, the heat from his body. She felt as if she were standing under a waterfall, trying to identify each individual water droplet. It couldn't be done. All she could do was to allow the emotions to wash over her, carrying her along in their wake.

She clutched his shoulders, her fingers biting into his muscles as he pushed her onto her back and leaned over her to reach for the condom on the table. His chest was bare inches from her mouth, and she raised her head and rubbed her face in the thick tangle of hair. It's rough texture scraped enticingly over her cheek. Burying her face in the dark cloud, she breathed deeply of the musky scent of him. He smelled so wonderful. And he felt even better; she absorbed the movement of his muscles as he fumbled with the packet.

Livvy gasped as his hand suddenly slipped between her legs and he gently probed her femininity. Her hands tightened convulsively around him. Suddenly her need for him bubbled up, drowning her last, lingering inhibitions. She wanted him. Now. Not later. Imperiously she tugged him over her, lifting her hips against his probing masculinity.

"We should…" Conal's muttered words echoed meaninglessly in her ears. She wanted action from him, not words. Words were imprecise things. The feel of him pushing against her was not. It was substantial. The most important thing that had ever happened to her.

Impatiently she wrapped her arms around his lean waist and tugged him downward. A glorious sense of excitement flowed through her as he pushed forward, slowly filling her.

A frantic sense of urgency blanked all thoughts from her mind as he began to move back and forth with powerful thrusts. Frantically she tried to slow her response. She wanted it to last longer. She wanted time….

Her entire body clenched and then shuddered as reaction ripped through her, tossing her into a blissful world that had no anchor in logic or common sense.

Livvy was slowly starting to surface through the maelstrom of pleasure when she felt Conal go rigid in her arms and then collapse bonelessly on her.

Livvy snuggled her face into his damp shoulder, too enervated to move. She felt as if she would never move again. It was strange, she thought foggily, as Conal rolled onto his side and, gathering her in his arms, cradling her against his chest. Usually fantasy was far better than reality. But in this case, the fantasy of making love to Conal didn't begin to compare to the reality. And the best part was they could do it again and again. Her thoughts dissolved into nothingness as she drifted off to sleep.

Five

Livvy muttered sleepily as the warmth of the tropical sun gently warmed her bare skin, making her feel boneless. She stretched luxuriously, relishing the feeling of well-being. She felt so wonderful. So absolutely...naked. She frowned uncertainly. Why was she lying on the beach naked?

Confused, she opened her eyes and found herself staring into Conal's dark eyes. His dark, watchful eyes. Livvy squirmed under his gaze, her knee accidentally brushing against the hairy roughness of his thigh. A melting sensation curled through her at the memory of how his thighs had felt against her own much-softer ones.

She felt her eyelids dropping under the weight of her memories. She wanted to make love to him again. To press kisses all over him, starting at his forehead and working her way downward. She wanted to bask in his warmth.

But what did Conal want? The thought chilled her escalating desire. Had making love to her once been enough for him? She peered up through her thick lashes at his still face. He was staring at her with an unreadable expression. Had he been disappointed with their lovemaking? Her toes curled in dismay at the thought. Frantically she tried to remember exactly what had happened, but she couldn't separate it into individual events. It was all a blur of heat and urgency and mind-boggling pleasure. She had been so caught up in her own responses that she hadn't paid much attention to what he was feeling. What he felt like, yes. But his reactions, no. Her shoulders slumped dispiritedly. What kind of a lover would he think she was? A selfish one. The only possible answer did nothing to raise her spirits.

What should she do about it? Apologize and tell him she would do better the next time? Suppose he said that he didn't want there to be a next time? Her skin crawled at the thought of dealing with a rejection like that while lying in bed naked with him. Rejections were best dealt with fully clothed with at least the length of an office desk between the parties.

"Are you going back to sleep?" Conal fought to keep the disappointment out of his voice. It was all he could do not to grab her and make love to her all over again. To lose himself in the wonder of their lovemaking.

Maybe she should say yes, Livvy considered. With luck Conal might get up and go downstairs, leaving her to regain her sense of balance without his distracting presence. Although, after his experience with her family last night, he probably wouldn't want to tackle them on his own. Not that she blamed him. An involuntary smile curved her lips at the memory of the expression on her uncle's face.

"What's so funny?" Conal asked.

"I was just remembering the look on Uncle Harry's face when you assumed that the men would clean things up just because the women had spent most of the day preparing all that food."

Conal winced at the reminder of his faux pas. He already knew that he didn't know how to fit into a real family, but it had been embarrassing to have the point underscored in front of everyone.

"They didn't have to stare at me like I'd just suggested we sacrifice a kid or two to the harvest gods," he muttered.

"They were all in shock," Livvy explained, when what she wanted to do was to take him in her arms and kiss away his disgruntled expression...to replace it with the intoxicating look of desire that had illuminated it last night. "The men, because another man questioned the status quo when it is so heavily tilted in their favor. The women were so surprised to hear a man admit that they might have an obligation around the house not involving a power tool that they didn't know how to react."

"Fair's fair," he said absently, rather startled to realize that in this instant at least he'd gained more points with Livvy by not fitting in with the rest of her family. Maybe she didn't want a husband in the traditional mold? Maybe she would be willing to take a chance on a man with no background in family living? No built-in prejudices as it were. Maybe he could find a way to compensate for his total lack of family experience? Maybe it wasn't the insurmountable obstacle he'd always believed it to be.

"So what has fairness ever had to do between husbands and wives?" Livvy broke into his racing thoughts. "Marriage is the most perfect example of how men have ordered the world for their own benefit that I've ever seen."

"Don't generalize."

"Generalize!" Livvy responded from the depths of countless lost arguments with her elderly relations. "What about my aunts and cousins? Most of them hold down jobs just like their husbands, and yet they're the ones expected to do the housework and take time off if one of the kids happens to get sick."

"If they don't like the way the chores in their marriages are divided, why don't they say something?"

"You said something last night. How much good did it do you?"

"But I'm an outsider," Conal said, ignoring the pain that tore through him at the admission. He didn't want lines drawn, with Livvy on the inside and him on the outside looking in. He wanted to be beside her, wherever that was.

"If one member of the relationship isn't happy, then it's up to the dissatisfied member to demand change," he said, dredging up the maxim from a long-ago college course on human relationships out of the depths of his memory.

Livvy weighed his words and found them comforting. All the more so because they neatly tallied with the way Conal behaved. As a boss he had never expected her to make his coffee or run his personal errands just because she was a woman, like several of her previous bosses had. He did his own dirty work. In fact, that aspect of his personality was the second thing she'd noticed about him—that he gave more than lip service to equality between the sexes in the workplace. She'd thought at the time that it would make him an ideal husband for a woman who valued her career.

Conal shrugged, and the sheet covering his chest slipped slightly, giving Livvy a distracting view of his broad chest. "The bottom line is that you can't change anyone's life but your own," he concluded.

Livvy opened her mouth to refute his simplistic view and then closed it again when she realized that, simplistic or not, he was right. She couldn't fix things for anyone else. The only life she could direct was her own. And the direction she wanted to aim it in at the moment was toward Conal's large body. She wanted to snuggle up to him and kiss him and see what developed.

But she simply didn't have the courage to make the first move. Despite the fact that the paralyzing shyness that had gripped her when she'd first woken up had mostly disappeared, she still didn't feel comfortable enough in her newfound role as Conal's lover to make any demands on him. In fact, she didn't feel comfortable at all. She felt unsure of herself and strangely young.

Livvy suppressed a sigh. She had achieved her heart's desire; she'd made love to Conal. But, unfortunately, it hadn't sated her compulsive desire for him as she'd hoped it would. It appeared to have merely whetted her appetite.

Maybe she should try to put things back on a normal footing between them in the hopes of gaining some time to become more comfortable in her new role. At least as near to normal as she was able to be with the memory of their lovemaking hanging between them. And that would be far easier to do if they weren't lying in bed naked together. Downstairs, around other people, it would be easier for her to try to recapture their former easy comradery.

"I guess we should get up," she offered. "Fern says there's a lot planned for today."

"Okay." Conal leaned back, laced his fingers together and put his hands behind his head.

Livvy gave herself a moment to relish the size and shape of his biceps before saying, "So get up."

"Ladies first."

Livvy blinked. There was no way in the world she could force herself to climb out of bed stark naked under his interested gaze. Even if she had a perfect body, which she most emphatically did not, she still couldn't do it.

"I don't want to go first," she muttered.

"Neither do I." The gleam of devilment in his eyes deepened and Livvy felt an answering glimmer of excitement spark to life.

"There, that's the perfect example of what I was talking about." Livvy tried to use words to combat her growing desire. "I told you what I wanted, and you refused to do it. So now what? Do we call a counselor to mediate?"

"Sounds rather kinky to me."

Livvy gritted her teeth in frustration. "Stop being facetious. I want to get up."

"I'm not stopping you." He gave her a virtuous smile that increased her sense of uncertainty. Conal in a teasing mood was highly unpredictable, and much as she wanted to see where it led, prudence demanded that she put some distance between them while she hopefully regained her perspective. Maybe she could simply wrap the sheet around herself and use it as a shield.

Matching the thought to action, Livvy tightened the sheet around her breasts and began to inch toward the side of the bed.

"Quit trying to steal the covers." Conal grabbed hold of the sheet.

Livvy stared down at his large hand, outlined against the pale pink floral pattern of the sheet, and felt a seething sense of frustration. If she yanked and he didn't let go, the sheet might rip and she could just imagine what Fern would have to say about that. Her sister would probably still be teasing her about her wild night of passion when she was as old as her great-grandmother.

Maybe she could catch him off balance. If he was expecting her to retreat, maybe she could get possession of the sheet by advancing. Not giving herself time to consider the wisdom of her idea, Livvy suddenly lunged at Conal, intending to shove him over the side of the bed, grab the sheet and sprint for the bathroom.

It didn't quite work out that way. She wound up sprawled half-across him, her face squashed into his chest. Slowly she raised her head and found herself gazing at his tantalizing lips.

"Does this mean you've changed your mind about getting up?" he asked.

"No," she muttered. "It means I'm about to trade in my long-held pacifistic beliefs and thump you!"

Conal laughed, and the sound poured enticingly into her ears while her body absorbed the impact of his shaking body. It was a potent reminder of how it had felt when he'd made love to her last night.

"You could always try, but I wouldn't give much for your chances," he said.

Livvy stared at his sparkling eyes, captivated by the humor she could see there, as well as annoyed at the smug awareness of his own physical superiority. He knew that he was impervious to any attempts on her part to wrest the sheet from him by force. And what was worse, he knew she knew it! But there was far more to strategy than brute force, Livvy encouraged herself.

Her thoughts scattered as Conal shifted slightly, and his hair-covered chest scraped abrasively across the tips of her breasts. Tremors coursed down her arms and collected in the pit of her stomach where they seemed to be holding a handball tourney.

She felt like someone who was trying to focus on a single thought while the television, the stereo and the radio were simultaneously blaring in her ear. It was impossible. And to make matters worse, on some level she didn't want to shut him out. She wanted to give in to the feelings he created. To sink down into the sensual pool that was lapping at her mind and make love to him again. Slowly, lingeringly, pausing to savor every nuance of his magnificent body.

But that would be appeasing her emotions at the expense of her mind, so she desperately fought her escalating desire. Her mind was emphatically telling her that while it was okay to make love to Conal, she absolutely had to keep control of the situation. And the only way she could get a handle on her emotions was by putting some space between them. Even if it was only the length of a room. She knew that if she ignored her mind's warning and listened to her emotions which were clambering for satisfaction, she would be setting a dangerous precedent. One that could only lead to trouble in the future. Big trouble. And she was already risking enough trouble by indulging her love for Conal to the extent she was.

She should leave, Livvy reminded herself. She should put some distance between her and Conal. Distance that hopefully would allow her to regain her perspective. To decide what would be the best thing to do and then do it instead of wavering back and forth between what she wanted to do and what she should be doing to further her long-range goals.

Deliberately she allowed her muscles to go slack, hoping that Conal would think she had given up. She gulped as her breasts seemed to flow against his hard chest. The sensation disconcerted her. Everything with Conal seemed so different. So unexpected. So brand-new. As if her own body had depths to it that she'd never suspected, and only Conal held the key to unlocking them.

Don't think about it now, she told herself, trying to concentrate on the more-immediate problem of how to escape the sensual trap that was sucking her deeper and deeper into its maw with her every breath.

Livvy rested her forehead against his chest as she tried to think. It was a tactical mistake. His chest hair rubbed abrasively against her skin, seeming to scrape away a great many of her inhibitions with it. She was fast reaching the point where she was oblivious to everything but her need for him. She had to get away before he realized how much more involved in their lovemaking she was than he. It would be too humiliating if he did.

Maybe he was ticklish, the idea suddenly occurred to her. Maybe she could give him a quick tickle, and when he laughed she could escape with the sheet. But where did one tickle a person for maximum effect? She had never before in her life purposefully tickled someone, but then she'd never been in quite such a tight corner before. Maybe she ought to try his chest? Or maybe she ought to try lower? Weren't men supposed to be more ticklish when they were aroused? She vaguely recalled the fact from an article she'd read once. Maybe... She shifted uncertainly and then gasped when she realized just how aroused he already was.

His waist, she struggled to concentrate on her plan. That seemed like a relatively safe part of his delectable anatomy to touch. Tentatively Livvy lightly tickled him. Nothing happened. She pushed a little harder with her fingertips, momentarily losing her concentration as she felt the firm give of his enticing flesh.

There was absolutely no response from him.

"What are you doing?" Conal asked curiously.

"Don't you have any nerve endings?" she demanded in frustration.

Conal chuckled. "I think you'll find that in the male the majority of nerve endings are to be found in—"

"I don't want to know." Livvy tried to head off a subject that was full of pitfalls. Compulsively attractive pitfalls.

"Then why'd you ask?"

Because I never learn, Livvy thought.

"I don't ask questions when I don't want answers," he added.

"Don't sound so blasted smug," she said, taking exception to his tone.

"Smug? Me? Would I sound smug?"

"Yes," she said tartly. "And, if you must know, I was trying to tickle you."

"Did you know that the ancient Chinese used tickling as a form of torture?"

"No. Now ask me if I care."

"I'd rather ask you why you're trying to do something so unsocial as to tickle me?"

"It isn't half as unsocial as your not getting out of bed first or letting me have the sheet. You, sir, are no gentleman!"

"I never claimed to be. From what I've seen, gentlemen usually get the short end of the stick."

"Instead, you've given me the short end of the stick!"

"No, just the short end of the sheet." He grinned at her, and despite the maddening quality of his smile, Livvy was unable to entirely suppress the answering smile that teased her lips.

Making a monumental effort to keep her mind on her

eventual goal, she decided to change tactics. Since she wasn't having any luck outtricking him, she would try outwaiting him. Conal was a very high-energy person. He wouldn't be able to put up with inactivity for long. He would get up and break the stalemate.

She deliberately allowed herself to relax, trying to ignore the way her body molded itself to the contours of his. She felt pliant, as if she were made of putty and could be reformed into anything she wanted to be. Or that Conal wanted her to be. She gulped in air. She was having a great deal of trouble keeping her eyelids open.

Livvy laid her head back down on his chest, relishing the raspy texture of his hair-covered skin against her cheek. If she lived to be a hundred, she didn't think she would ever cease to marvel at the differences between men and women. It seemed so strange that nature could make them so different and yet so complementary.

She licked the tight bud of a nipple buried in the cloud of dark hair. A bright curl of satisfaction shot through her when Conal jerked as if she'd laid a lit match across his skin. She opened one eye and peered at the red numbers on the bedside clock. They had eight minutes before they had to get up, if they were to make it to her grandparents' house on time.

Drat it all, anyway, Livvy thought in frustration. Why did their weekend have to be so tightly scheduled? Why couldn't they have some time to themselves? Time to do what she really wanted to do. Lie here all day long. Conal made an absolutely fantastic mattress.

"What are you doing?" Conal's words stirred the hairs on the top of her head, and she shivered.

"Thinking up advertising copy," she said brightly, trying to sound a lot more sophisticated than she felt.

"Advertising copy?" he repeated. "We don't handle X-rated accounts."

"No," Livvy said, pressing her ear harder against his chest so that she could hear the heavy thudding of his heart. It beat with a slow, steady rhythm that was probably the pride of his doctor.

She shifted slightly, and his heartbeat accelerated slightly. Now *that* was interesting, she thought, wondering how fast she could make his heart race.

"No, what?" Conal's voice sounded slightly strained. She had no idea what he was asking about. Nor could she even remember what they'd been talking about. Abstract ideas seemed virtually impossible to hold on to when her body was pressed so close to his. It was as if her emotions were overloading her senses so much that there was no room left in her mind for rational thought.

Tentatively she trailed her fingers down the side of his chest, probing the hardness of his ribs beneath his taut skin. To her pleasure, his heartbeat escalated. Encouraged, she took a deep breath to gather her courage, and then almost lost sight of her purpose when her breasts swelled with reaction to the added pressure. Focus, she urged herself. Focus on driving Conal nuts.

Her hand dipped lower, and she grasped his heated manhood in her hand almost jumping when his heart began to race. "What are you doing!"

"What am I doing?" she repeated with mock incredulity.

"What part of this don't you understand?"

"Where you're concerned, nothing," he said hoarsely.

"Well, this is easy enough to understand." She rubbed her fingers down the length of him, shivering at his hard rigidity. "I'm conducting a scientific investigation."

"Tell me—" he twisted beneath her touch "—does it

have something to do with how much frustration a man can take before he goes stark-raving mad?''

She giggled happily, having the feeling she'd unexpectedly gained the upper hand. "To go along with your being stark naked? Actually, I'm simply tracking the rate of your heartbeat."

"My heartbeat?" he repeated uncomprehendingly.

"Uh-huh." Livvy nodded, and the slight movement of her body on his sent a wave of pleasure through her. "Do you know that when I do this—'' she tightened her fingers around his heated length and he jerked in reaction "—your heartbeat speeds up. It's a fascinating cause-and-effect relationship."

"I'll show you another cause-and-effect relationship," his deep voice rasped over her nerves.

"Oh?" She raised her head and peered into his eyes. They were so dark they looked black, and the pupils were huge. She licked her dry lips as she watched the tiny silvery lights deep in them sparkling. She felt as if she could fall into his eyes. Fall into them and never surface.

"Do that again," Conal ordered, and Livvy obediently tightened her fingers. To her shock and utter delight, he suddenly tipped her onto her back and covered her large body with his. His weight pressed her into the soft mattress, but instead of feeling squashed, she felt protected. Safe.

She gasped as she felt his warmth push against her, and then every muscle in her body clenched as he drove into her welcoming body with one powerful surge. She trembled at the feel of his heat inside her, and tiny tremors began to spiral through her.

"Now that is a much better cause-and-effect relationship," he said in satisfaction.

He was wrong, Livvy thought dreamily. They'd left

science behind and were now firmly in the realm of fantasy. This was the stuff of which dreams were made.

She twisted her head as he pushed forward, and the unforgiving red dials of the clock eyed her malevolently. "It's late," she muttered.

"Far too late," Conal agreed.

"No, I mean we have to get up in—" She made a valiant effort to focus on the time. It was one of the hardest things she'd ever done. Time didn't seem to have any meaning for her. Nothing seemed really important but the feel of him buried deep inside her.

Conal turned to look at the clock, and his movement sent a gasp of reaction racing through her.

"How much time do we have?" he asked, as his hands slipped beneath her hips and he lifted her against him, tightening the spiral of excitement building in her.

Time? The word echoed in Livvy's ears. "What time is it now?" she finally asked.

"Eight fifty-six."

"Eight fifty-six," she repeated trying to subtract it from nine o'clock. She couldn't. The numbers slid through her mind, becoming wedged between the desire gripping her.

"Nine o'clock," she finally said. "We have to get up at nine o'clock or—" The words ended on a sigh as he slipped his hand between them and, capturing her nipple, gently tugged on it.

"I probably don't have time to do this," he murmured, and Livvy twisted beneath him as a slightly frantic feeling engulfed her. She felt as if she were caught in the grip of something that he couldn't contain.

"If I haven't time to do that, I suppose I haven't time to do this, either?" He bent his head and captured one taut nipple in his mouth.

Livvy moaned and instinctively reached for him. Her

trembling fingers grabbed his head, holding him close. She felt as if she would die if he stopped. Nothing else had any meaning to her. Not her sister or the need to get to her grandmother's. Those things were totally insignificant beside the overwhelming sense of urgency which had wrapped itself around her.

"Then I guess I'll just have to hurry," Conal said, and purposefully thrust forward again.

To Livvy's shock, her whole body clenched and then exploded in a paroxysm of reaction. She pressed her face in his chest to stifle the moans she could feel bubbling between her lips. His arms tightened around her with bruising force as he suddenly went rigid and then collapsed on her.

"We still have a minute to spare." Conal gasped the words out.

How could he find the energy to say anything? She felt as if she would never move a muscle again. As if she never wanted to move again. She nuzzled her face against him in contentment.

"Hey, Aunt Livvy?" Bobby's voice drifted through the closed door. "Mom said to tell ya it's getting late."

"Thank you." Livvy made a monumental effort to break free of the lethargy that held her in its grasp.

"And Dad said we shouldn't be in any hurry to rush Conal out to the reunion 'cause once he's met all Mom's weird relatives he might decide to call off the wedding. And Mom said that her family wasn't any weirder than his family and—"

"Thanks, Bobby." Livvy hurriedly cut him off before he related something truly embarrassing.

Conal felt his spirits lift at Bobby's words. It sounded

as if Bill had his own problems relating to Livvy's family,
too. It wasn't just he who felt so out of place. And yet
Bill had seemed to fit in last night. The thought fed his
fragile sense of hope.

Six

Livvy nervously tucked the hem of her teal silk shirt a little more securely into her beige slacks as she made her way downstairs. She didn't know why Conal's lovemaking made her feel so unsure of herself as if she didn't really know herself half as well as she'd always thought she did. But it didn't bother her enough to give up making love to Conal while she had the chance.

She paused on the bottom step as a flood of evocative memories made her skin tingle. There was no incentive on earth powerful enough to make her give up Conal's lovemaking one second before she had to.

"Morning, Livvy. Sorry if Bobby disturbed you," Bill's clipped voice jerked her out of her thoughts, and she blinked, focusing on her brother-in-law with an effort.

"S'okay," she lied politely, frowning slightly as she got a good look at him. His features were drawn, and the muscles in his jaw were clenched as if he were holding back harsh words.

"Is something the matter, Bill?" Livvy asked uncertainly. She'd known him as long as she could remember, and he'd always been unfailingly cheerful, at times annoyingly so. Livvy couldn't ever remember him looking as grim as he did now.

"What could possibly be the matter?" Bill's bitter voice was a parody of his normal, easygoing tone.

Livvy started to answer him and then paused as she remembered several things Fern had said yesterday. Things that she had wondered about at the time. Could he and Fern have had a fight? It seemed unlikely. Livvy had always thought them the most perfectly matched couple she'd ever met. As well as one of the happiest.

But then, things weren't always what they seemed. Her sense of disquiet increased. She'd been madly in love with Conal for over a year now, and none of her friends or family had had the vaguest inkling of the fact.

"Bill," Livvy said slowly, having no idea what she wanted to say. She didn't want to pry, but maybe she could help, provided there really was something wrong. She tried to still her growing sense of unease. She could simply be projecting her own insecurities onto Bill.

"Livvy, there you are." Fern stuck her head out of the kitchen. "Come keep me company while I put the finishing touches on my contribution to the family feast," she said, totally ignoring Bill's presence.

Without a word, Bill turned and walked into the living room, his gait stiff.

With a last, doubtful look at Bill's rigid back, Livvy followed Fern out to the kitchen.

Sitting down at the table, Livvy thoughtfully watched Fern's jerky movements as she stirred the potato salad she was making. "Not to put my nose in where it isn't wanted, but is something the matter between you and Bill?" Livvy finally asked.

"The matter? Why, what could possibly be the matter? We..." Fern paused as her lip began to quiver. She gulped and then blurted out, "Oh, Livvy, I just don't know what to do!"

"About what?" Conal's deep voice scraped over Livvy's nerve endings, and she looked up to see him standing in the doorway eyeing the coffeepot.

Livvy stood up to get him a cup, but he waved her back down and got it himself. She watched, fascinated, as his lips that just minutes before had been caressing her tingling body curved around the rim of the navy mug.

Conal took a deep, reviving sip and turned to Fern. "You were saying?"

"Nothing important," Fern muttered.

Conal felt his flesh tighten at her dismissive words. It was as if she'd judged his lack of experience in personal relationships and instantly dismissed him as having anything of worth to contribute.

Conal forced himself to calmly take another sip of coffee. When he raised his head, his eyes met Livvy's, and she grimaced ruefully at him. As if her inquires had been brushed aside, too. As if they were ranged together.

He felt his tense muscles slowly begin to unknot.

"Fern, we aren't trying to pry," Livvy said.

"Oh, I know. It's just that— Oh, hell! Why should I keep it a secret? Everyone will know sooner or later. Bill's been offered a promotion. One he really wants, and it has a big raise with it."

"Then why are the two of you looking like the IRS decided to audit your tax return?" Livvy asked in confusion.

"Because the job is in Atlanta. Georgia!" she added as if they might not understand.

"A very cosmopolitan place," Conal offered tentatively.

"You don't understand!" Fern wailed. "If we move away, I'll lose everything I've worked for. Here I have my own classroom, the grade I want and tenure. In Atlanta I'll have to start all over again with substitute teaching, and I hate substitute teaching."

"What happens if Bill doesn't take the job?" Conal asked when Livvy simply sat there looking shocked.

"His manager warned Bill that the company wouldn't offer him a promotion again," Fern admitted. "This will be the third one he's turned down."

Livvy winced. "Tough."

"But it isn't like they're going to fire him or anything," Fern insisted. "He can stay right where he is doing exactly what he has been until he retires."

"And getting more frustrated every year," Conal said, chilled by the picture Fern's words evoked.

"What about Fern's frustrations?" Livvy automatically defended her sister, caught off balance by Conal's seeming willingness to sacrifice Fern's hard-won gains in her own job. Would he be that dismissive of his wife's career if it interfered with something he wanted? Would he expect that his wife would be the one to automatically give in and give up?

She'd always found him very supportive of her career, but then she worked for him, she reminded herself. She made a great deal of money for his company. Could Conal be one of those men who believed in working wives as long as it wasn't his wife? Livvy didn't know. Which meant that she also didn't know what would happen if she somehow did manage to convince him to marry her and they had children? Children took a lot of time and effort. Would Conal automatically assume that she should put her career on hold while the kids were little? The appalling thought made Livvy want to scream. She may have been making all her plans based on an assumption that wasn't true.

"Livvy, I—" Fern broke off as Bill appeared in the doorway.

"You've got a call, Conal," Bill said. "It's a woman. She said she called over at Marie's, and Marie gave her this number."

Conal set down his coffee cup and looked around the kitchen for a phone.

"There's one in the living room," Livvy told him. "Come on. I'll show you." She was glad to momentarily escape both her own unsettling thoughts and the emotionally charged atmosphere that seemed to vibrate between Bill and Fern.

"There." Livvy pointed to the phone on the end table beside the couch. She started to leave to give him some privacy for his call, even though what she really wanted to do was stay and eavesdrop. To find out if the answering service had given the woman her mother's number or if Conal would tell the woman where he would be spending the weekend.

To her relief, Conal gestured her into a chair as he picked up the receiver.

Livvy felt her muscles imperceptibly loosen as she listened to his end of the conversation. It was business. The caller seemed to want Conal to write some television spots.

"I understand that but... No, I don't think...yes, goodbye." Conal hung up the phone and turned to Livvy, his expression thoughtful.

"That was a Miss Evert from Congresswoman Darnell's office. It seems the congresswoman has slipped in the latest opinion polls and wants to hire a new ad agency to do some television spots for her."

Livvy frowned. "But why us? We've never done any political ads before."

"She said we were recommended to her by one of our former clients, although she didn't say which one. What do you think of the idea?"

Livvy absently tucked her hair back behind her right ear as she considered his question, and Conal felt his body clench as he remembered the silky feel of her hair against his own fingers. Remembered the faint scent of some kind of flowers that he'd smelled when he'd buried his face in it. Remembered...business. He pulled his mind out of the quagmire of sensuality that was sucking him down. Concentrate on business, not on making love to Livvy, he ordered himself.

"I don't like what political advertising has descended to," she said slowly. "More often than not, it's character assassination rather than an attempt to sway the voters to your beliefs."

"It doesn't have to be."

Livvy grimaced. "No, and mankind doesn't have to fight wars, but I'm still not looking for an outbreak of peace anytime soon."

"You're against doing it?"

"It's your agency," she said, not wanting him to think that she expected him to pay more attention to her opinion simply because he'd made love to her. She couldn't bear it if he were to believe that she was the type of woman who traded sex for business concessions.

"Since when has that ever stopped you from voicing an opinion before?" he asked dryly.

"That was different," she muttered.

"Why?"

Livvy gritted her teeth together in frustration. She didn't want to talk about what they'd shared. It was too new, too fragile and far too precious to risk trying to analyze. But unfortunately, when Conal wanted an answer, he could be worse than a pit bull attacking a T-bone steak. Livvy glanced toward the hallway. There was no sign of Fern or Bill. "Because of what…we…" She gestured ineffectively.

Conal's dark eyebrows shot up. "Do you mean to tell me that you intend to treat me differently just because I allowed you to take liberties with my body? Does this mean you no longer respect me?"

Livvy stared at him incredulously. Liberties? Respect? Those were the woman's lines and thirty years out-of-date besides. What was Conal doing spouting them?

"I think this means that you've taken leave of your senses," she finally said.

"Does that mean that you still respect me?" The wicked gleam in his eyes intensified, stirring something deep within her. She wanted to grab him close and press her lips to his. To trace over the firm line of his jaw first with her fingertips and then with her lips. She wanted to savor the distinctly masculine texture of his skin. But she couldn't. Fern's living room was not the place to kiss Conal the way she wanted to. Leisurely. Thoroughly.

"You are making the assumption that I respected you in the first place," Livvy said. "Quit talking nonsense."

"I'm not so sure it is nonsense," he said thoughtfully. "But to get back to your objections. Don't you want to try to change things?"

"One person?" she scoffed.

"No," Conal's voice deepened enticingly. "Two people. The two of us together."

Together. Livvy tasted the word and found it sweet as well as very seductive. But he was speaking about work. She shivered slightly as she remembered his automatic assumption that Fern should sacrifice the gains she'd made in her own career to advance Bill's.

Livvy swallowed uneasily. What would happen to her love for Conal if she were forced to spend her days in an apartment with no one but an infant for company? What would happen to her sanity? Get a grip on yourself, she ordered her skittery mind. You haven't even gotten a declaration of love out of the man, let alone a proposal of marriage. Concentrate on what you know to be facts.

"Livvy!" Fern stormed into the living room, followed by a glowering Bill. "You think I'm right, don't you? Tell Bill he's being selfish."

Livvy winced at the unhappiness she could see seething in Fern's eyes. An unhappiness that was echoed in Bill's.

Helplessly Livvy glanced at Conal. She did think her sister was right, but she could also see Bill's side of it. Having to turn down a great job that you'd worked hard for would be difficult. Especially if you knew that you wouldn't get another chance.

"There's an old Chinese saying that only fools take sides between a husband and wife, and Livvy's no fool," Conal made an effort to defuse the tension for Livvy's sake.

"She's my sister!" Fern insisted. "What's more, she's a woman."

"I noticed." Conal's deep voice vibrated in Livvy's chest, and she flushed.

"This isn't funny!" Fern's glare was about equally divided between Conal and her husband. She scowled as the front door burst open and then was slammed shut. A second later footsteps sounded as Bobby pounded up the stairs.

"If Bobby doesn't start using the back door..." Fern snapped.

A furious pounding on the front door interrupted her. "Who on earth is that?" Fern looked blankly at Livvy, who shrugged.

"I'm not sure I want to know," Livvy said. "Whoever it is sounds pretty upset. Tell me, when was the last time you paid your paperboy?"

"I know you're in there. Open up!" A deep male voice bellowed.

"That sounds like Carl from down the street," Bill said as he went to answer the front door trailed by the other three.

Livvy glanced up the stairs to see a frightened looking Bobby peering around the edge of the bathroom door. Obviously he was at the root of this, but what could he have done to have angered an adult so badly?

Bill swung open the front door to reveal a sniveling boy about half Bobby's size and a man who looked like the before shots of an ad for a diet program. Livvy's eyes instinctively swung to Conal's well-muscled form. While Conal looked like the after shots.

"Did you want something, Carl?" Fern finally asked when no one else said anything.

"Damn right I do!" the man bellowed. "I'm going to beat the hell out of that brat of yours."

Bill blinked as if trying to mentally shift gears to cope with yet another crisis. "What are you talking about?" he finally asked.

"Your kid, that's what I'm talking about! He attacked my poor little Mike!"

Livvy winced. Didn't the man have any tone below a bellow?

"Bobby, come down here," Bill called up the stairs.

There was a moment's silence. It was punctuated by the pathetic-sounding whimpers that Mike was uttering, with what Livvy suspected was practiced ease, before Bobby appeared at the top of the stairs and slowly trailed down them.

"Bobby, what's all this about?" Bill asked.

"I told you what he did," Carl began, but Bill cut him off.

"I asked my son."

Bobby eyed the angry Carl uncertainly. "I only hit Mike cause he told me to." Bobby pointed a shaky finger toward Conal.

Conal frowned and took a closer look at the sniveling Mike.

"Conal told you to beat him up?" Bill asked in disbelief.

Bobby shook his head emphatically. "I didn't beat him up. He's too big. I just hit him and ran home."

"Bobby, is Mike the bully who's been bothering you?" Conal asked.

Bobby nodded with a scared glance at Mike. "He waits at the end of the corner every morning and steals my lunch money," he blurted out.

"That's a lie!" Carl yelled. "My son isn't a thief."

"But why didn't you tell me, Bobby?" Bill's voice sounded strange to Livvy. Almost as if he were...hurt?

Bobby squirmed. "'Cause when I told the teacher on him, Mike said he'd beat me up even worse if I told you or Mom. I didn't mean to tell him." Bobby gestured toward Conal. "It just kind of slipped out, and he said that I should hit him."

"I said he should hit him *back*," Conal corrected. "One should always stand up to bullies."

"My son is not a bully!" Carl yelled. "He's a victim."

"Ah, the lament of present-day America," Livvy said. "Everyone is a victim. No one is responsible for his own actions."

"Livvy!" Fern frowned at her. "This isn't funny. Your fiancé is advocating violence!"

Conal eyed Fern uncertainly. How could she object to his telling Bobby to defend himself? What did she expect the kid to do? Allow himself to be used as a punching bag? He shifted uncertainly. He didn't understand her reasoning at all. But then, he didn't know anything about raising kids, he conceded. Maybe there was something basic he was missing.

"You'll be hearing from my lawyer!" Carl added one final threat and then stomped off the porch, trailed by his still-sniffling son.

"Oh, dear." Fern watched them go. "Do you suppose he means it?"

"I sincerely doubt it," Livvy said comfortingly. "He sounds like just as big a bully as his son. Come on, let's finish cleaning up the kitchen before we're late for Grandma's."

"But I still say that violence never solves anything." Fern shot a reproachful glance at Conal as she left.

Livvy paused a moment to give Conal a quick kiss, unable to resist the urge to try to comfort him. He looked so confused. As well he might, Livvy thought dejectedly. This weekend at her sister's seemed expressly designed to convince Conal that his decision to avoid marriage was the right one. As well as to make her doubt her basic premise that Conal was a man with whom she could have it all—marriage, children and a demanding career.

Livvy instinctively pressed closer to the warmth of his body. Anticipation shivered through her, scattering her doubts and uncertainties. With a last smile for Conal, Livvy followed her sister out to the kitchen.

"Are you mad at me, too, Daddy?" Bobby asked hesitantly.

Bill shook his head. "No. Conal's right. Sometimes you have to stand up for yourself. If that involves smacking a bully then smack him. But if I ever find out you started the fight, you'll be grounded for the rest of your natural life, understand? Now go ask your mother if there's anything she wants you to do before we leave."

"Yes, sir," Bobby muttered and scurried out to the kitchen as Livvy returned.

"Thanks for helping Bobby." Bill bit out the words as if they pained him. "If I hadn't been so caught up in my own problems..." He rubbed the back of his neck in frustration. "Oh hell, what's the use? I can't seem to get anything right." He turned to Livvy. "I need to think. Tell Fern I'll come out to the farm later. There's no way I can face all her relatives now and pretend that everything is just fine."

He stalked out of the house, and a moment later Conal heard the sound of his truck pulling out of the driveway.

So his initial impression had been right. Bill wasn't entirely comfortable around Livvy's family, Conal thought. Which meant that having been raised in a middle-class family didn't automatically give one the ability to fit into any family. Nor apparently did a so-called normal upbringing automatically give a person the ability to solve personal problems.

And not only that but Bill had also totally missed the fact that Bobby was being bullied at school. Bill's normal background hadn't made him sensitive to his son's problems. What's more, Fern's normal background certainly hadn't resulted in her giving her son any practical advice. That had been left to him.

Conal felt a brief spurt of satisfaction that was promptly drowned in confusion when he also remembered that Fern and Bill had some areas of disagreement about the best way to raise their son. Disagreements that they hadn't solved in six years. But why not?

He sighed. He didn't know that, but he did know there was a whole lot more to family relationships than he'd ever suspected when he'd been on the outside looking in. Compromise seemed to be much more important than he'd originally thought. And relationships seemed to involve a great deal of hard work, much like learning the intricacies of a professional football defense. He'd learned how to do that, he encouraged himself. Learned it well enough to be voted best at his position eight years running. Perhaps he could learn to be a husband to Livvy.

But what about learning to be a father? The thought gave him pause. Could he learn to be a father? Did he even want to learn to be a father? He wasn't sure. He wasn't even sure if Livvy wanted children. Surely if that had been her goal in life, she would have married long before now. And she hadn't. She'd devoted all her time and energy to her career.

Maybe he ought to try to find out if she wanted children. But carefully, obliquely. He didn't want to accidentally push her into making a sudden decision about his worth as a husband. Not when he didn't know how she would choose.

Conal ran his fingers through his hair in frustration at yet one more uncertainty he had to deal with. He needed to focus on the positive, he told himself. And it didn't get more positive than making love to Livvy.

Maybe he could find a way to get her by herself long enough to steal a kiss or two sometime during the day. He felt his lips tingle at the thought of kissing her again. Of his tongue dipping into her mouth and tasting her sweetness. And if he were really lucky, he would find enough privacy to slip his hand beneath that silky blouse of hers and caress the warm fullness of her fantastic breasts. His fingers clenched involuntarily at the thought.

"Conal, Aunt Livvy says where is you?" Bobby yelled from the kitchen doorway.

Conal sighed and reluctantly headed for the kitchen, not looking forward to having Fern give him reproachful looks. But then, Livvy was there, too, he remembered and his steps automatically quickened.

Seven

"It's the next turnoff on your right," Livvy instructed Conal. "You can't see the farmhouse from the road."

Conal shot her a speculative look, trying to imagine her living on a farm. He paid for his curiosity when the car hit a gigantic chuck hole and swerved to his left. His large hands instinctively tightened around the steering wheel, righting it.

"Doesn't Pennsylvania ever pave any of their roads?" he complained.

"Not according to my grandfather. Of course, he's also convinced that the Communists really won the Cold War and are busily redistributing the country's wealth through taxes."

Conal chuckled. "What does he grow?"

"Only flowers and veggies these days. Except for an acre or so around the house, he gave all the farmland to my uncle Henry years ago when he retired."

"So you never lived on the farm?" Conal asked, intensely curious about every aspect of her life.

"Nope, I was born in Mom's house and never lived anywhere else until I went away to college at Penn State. There." She gestured to the slight cut through the heavy stand of red-gold maples. "That's our road." Conal obediently turned.

"We seem to be among the last arrivals." Conal gestured toward the number of people sitting on the wide front porch. He tried to ignore his fears that today would be simply another replay of last night, when everything and everyone seemed expressly designed to point out to Livvy that he didn't belong. That he was different.

Parking the rental car beside a beat-up pickup, Conal got out and opened the door for Livvy.

"That's a great-looking car you got there, Conal," one of the elderly men he'd met yesterday, whose name escaped him, offered.

Conal grabbed the innocuous conversational gambit. "It handles well, too."

"Always wanted one of those Mercedes," Uncle Harry said. "Mind if I ask you what it cost?"

"I don't know," Conal said. "It's only rented. I don't own a car."

"You don't own a car!" Every single male eye stared at him in a combination of horror, disbelief and pity.

"Lad, you should have better sense than to spend all your money on a fancy diamond just to impress a woman," Uncle Harry lectured him.

Conal blinked, completely taken aback by their interpretation of his words. They actually thought he was broke. That he had no more sense than to spend his last dime to impress Livvy. He glanced at her, fascinated by the way her eyes were brimming with the laughter she was struggling to contain. And they would be right, he conceded. He would not only spend his last dime on Livvy, he would also mortgage his future if she asked him to.

"I'm not that expensive, Uncle Harry," Livvy said. "And you guys aren't thinking. Why would anyone want a car in New York City? It's far easier to take a taxi."

"Livvy, quit gossiping out there and come and introduce Conal to your grandmother. She's been waiting all morning to meet him," Marie called through the screen door.

Taking a deep breath, Conal followed Livvy into the house. The day wouldn't last forever, he encouraged himself. Sooner or later, they would return to the privacy of their bedroom and he would be able to make love to Livvy all over again. At least, he fervently hoped he would.

He glanced down at Livvy, his eyes lingering on the way her inky black hair curled around her creamy cheeks. His breathing shortened as he remembered the soft brush of her hair across his chest when she'd kissed him. He'd never realized just how provocative her hair was before, because in the office she always wore it pulled back in some kind of bun.

Feeling his body's instinctive reaction to his thoughts, Conal tried to distract himself by focusing on the colorful bouquet of dahlias on the antique upright piano.

"So, this is the man you finally settled on, Livvy?" An elderly woman addressed them from an overstuffed chair, which seemed to dwarf her tiny frame.

Livvy kissed her grandmother's cheek. "I missed you last night, Grandma. This is Conal Sutherland. Conal, this is my Grandmother Donagher."

"How do you do?" Conal said, uncomfortably reminded of Bobby by her unwinking stare.

"Marie says you work in New York City like Livvy?" Grandma Donagher said. "Are you sure you earn enough to support a wife? New York is a ruinously expensive city."

"Mother!" Marie squawked. "You can't ask the man how much he makes."

"You must not be listening, Marie. I just did."

"I don't need a man to support me," Livvy hurriedly interjected. "I can support myself."

"I can afford her." Conal swallowed a grin. The old woman was beginning to remind him of Livvy in one of her more determined moods. "I can support you, too, if it comes to that."

"If what I read about Social Security heading for bankruptcy is right, it might well!" Grandma Donagher shot back.

"You aren't one of these modern men who don't like kids, are you?" she returned to the attack.

It wasn't that he didn't like children; Conal mentally scrambled for something he could say that wasn't an outright lie. He liked them just fine, in the abstract. It was when he had to deal with them one-on-one that he ran into problems. The very thought of being responsible for turning someone like Bobby into a civilized member of society made his blood run cold. If he found out that Livvy did want children... His mind shied away from the disheartening thought.

Livvy glanced at Conal, her attention caught by his arrested expression. A feeling of disquietude dripped through her as she remembered how stiff Conal had been with Bobby. Could Fern have been right? Might Conal really not like kids? An image of a darling little boy with Conal's brown hair and mischievous grin floated through her mind. Surely he wouldn't object to just one?

Stop it! Livvy yanked her imagination up short. She wasn't really engaged to Conal, even if she wanted to be. Before worrying about how to convince him to give fatherhood a try, she first had to convince him to commit to matrimony—a goal that she feared was getting farther and farther away from her the longer he was around her family.

"It isn't so much that I don't like them," Conal finally said, "as it is that I don't have any experience with them."

"An only child, are you?" Grandma Donagher said sympathetically.

"I have no idea," Conal admitted. "I was left on a doorstep when I was just a few days old. I was raised in an orphanage."

An orphanage! Livvy stared at him in dumbfounded shock. Conal didn't come from a sophisticated background? He didn't have any family of his own? She felt an urge to throw her arms around him and protect him. Protect him from what? She mocked her impulse. He had a successful career, plenty of money, scores of friends and was well respected by his colleagues. He didn't need anything from her.

"You poor boy! How awful for you," Marie blurted out, and then blushed as if she'd said something she shouldn't have.

Livvy empathized with her mother's confusion. She wasn't sure what she should say, either, about Conal's totally unexpected revelation. Maybe saying nothing was best, she finally decided. Nothing she could say would make any difference. And if she said too much he might think that his lack of family mattered to her. And it didn't. She didn't care who Conal's parents had been or what they'd done. All she cared about was Conal.

"It doesn't matter, lad." Grandma Donagher patted Conal on the hand. "You'll have all of Livvy's family once you're married. And when is that happy day to be?" She slipped the question in.

"Grandma, we just got engaged," Livvy said to deflect her. "Give us a chance to get to know each other."

"Engaged couples know each other all too well these days," Grandma Donagher replied tartly.

"I promise you'll be the first to know when we set a date," Conal said.

"Yes, but…" Grandma Donagher paused as the pager in his pocket sounded. "What was that?"

"Conal's pager," Livvy said as he pulled it out and looked at it.

"It says it's urgent that I call back," he murmured. "It's a New York City area code, but I don't recognize the number. Do you?" He showed it to Livvy.

"No." Livvy shook her head.

"That's terrible," Marie said in outrage. "Bothering a man on a Saturday."

"That's the kind of job Conal has," Livvy pointed out. "He owns his own business and has to be available to his clients when they need him, no matter how inconvenient it is."

"Your dear father never worked weekends," Marie said doubtfully.

"Every job has its drawbacks, Marie," Grandma Donagher said. "Conal, you can use the phone in our bedroom. There shouldn't be anyone there. Livvy, show him where it is."

"Thank you," Conal said, grabbing the excuse to escape for a few minutes from everyone's curious eyes. He hated the pity he'd seen on their faces when he'd mentioned his childhood. Although Livvy hadn't seemed to pity him. She hadn't turned a hair at his revelation. A growing warmth spread through him, helping to ease his tense muscles, as he followed Livvy through the crowded house into a small bedroom in the back.

"There." Livvy pointed to the phone on the bedside table.

Conal barely noticed it. He was too busy noticing the bed. He wanted to grab her, tumble her down on it and kiss her until she couldn't think about anything but him. Of nothing but the feel and the taste of him.

A burst of laughter drifted in through the open window, and he regretfully discarded the idea. He couldn't risk it here. Anyone might walk in and find them.

After the phone call, he promised himself, he would suggest a walk through the woods. Through the empty woods. Maybe he could find a fallen log for them to sit on and... He shook his thoughts free of his increasingly erotic thoughts. The purpose of the walk was to get information, he reminded himself. To try to find out if she wanted children or not. Not, he fervently hoped, because that would make his task of convincing her to take a chance on him as a husband much easier. But first the call.

"Conal Sutherland here," he said when he reached the number.

Livvy watched as he chewed his lower lip, something he had a habit of doing when he was concentrating.

"I'm certainly gratified by your confidence in our agency, but— Yes, but— That would be fine. Goodbye." Conal hung up and stared blankly at the receiver for a moment.

"Problems?" Livvy asked.

"No," Conal said slowly. "It's a compliment really. That was the congresswoman herself with a pitch for us to do the television spots. You remember those ads we did for that computer chain last spring?''

Livvy nodded. "They were pretty good, if I do say so myself.''

"The owner of the computer chain is a big supporter of the congresswoman, and he recommended us. It would be a chance to branch out into a whole new area of advertising, and she did pretty much offer us a free hand...." Conal muttered as if thinking aloud.

"Hmm," Livvy murmured noncommittally. She had far more interesting things she would rather be doing than considering advertising contracts. She peered up at Conal from underneath her lashes. The sun coming in through the window had bathed him in a golden light that reminded her of the halo surrounding Abraham in the picture near the baptistry of her church.

She squinted slightly, trying to imagine Conal as a patriarch. It was surprisingly easy. Conal was intelligent, kind and well organized. He would be a natural as a patriarch. At least he would, once he got over his stiffness around kids. If his reserve around Bobby really was just stiffness and not symptomatic of something deeper. Such as a real dislike of kids.

But she'd never seen any evidence that he disliked anyone, she encouraged herself. Let alone a whole segment of the population. No, she tried to quiet her doubts. Conal's unease around children was undoubtedly caused by his upbringing. Once he got to know some kids he'd undoubtedly feel different. A vision of Bobby's youthful tormentor flashed through her mind, and she winced. Once Conal got to know some normal kids, he would feel different.

Although... Could it be that he hadn't married because he didn't like kids? Or could it be that he was just waiting until he got the agency well established before finding himself a wife? Were all his anti-marriage comments just red herrings designed to discourage the women he knew from viewing him as husband material until he was ready to take the plunge? Livvy gritted her teeth against the irrational rage that suddenly engulfed her at the thought of Conal standing at the altar with some strange woman.

Desperately she tried to force the feeling back into the depths of her mind, but it kept leaking out. She might know that simply having made love to Conal didn't give her any rights where he was concerned, but unfortunately her emotions didn't seem to be getting the message. They felt very possessive about Conal. Disquietingly possessive. As if his having made love to her had in some way committed him to her. Yet intellectually she knew that he hadn't uttered one word to her that she could possibly take as commitment. An impotent sense of frustration seeped through her.

"Are you all right?" Conal peered into her tense face.

"Why shouldn't I be?" Despite her efforts to control her feelings, a little of her tension seeped into her voice.

"Because you're looking as if you wanted to hit something," he said dryly. "If I weren't a lot bigger than you, I'd be worried."

Livvy looked down her nose at him. "Haven't you ever heard of David and Goliath?"

"I've heard lots of things, and I don't believe most of them."

"You can believe that size isn't everything."

"Ha! Platitudes aside, what is it going to take to convince you that in a physical struggle, you are as good as unarmed?"

Livvy stared into his laugh-filled eyes, and a surge of excitement, heavily tinged with a desire to show him that he shouldn't underestimate her, coursed through her. This morning had shown her that he was certainly right that in a straight test of strength between them she stood no chance, but it had also shown her that it was a lot of fun to try. Besides, victory didn't always go to the strong. Sometimes it went to the sneaky.

Casually turning as if she intended to go, Livvy suddenly pivoted and launched herself at him, intending to catch him off balance and topple him onto the bed. With luck she could steal a quick kiss and then beat a hasty retreat before he could retaliate.

Like so many of her plans where Conal was concerned, it didn't go quite the way she intended. She landed against him, all right, but he not only didn't topple onto the bed, he also didn't budge by so much as an inch. She found herself plastered against his chest, her nose pressed into his neck. Self-indulgently she took a deep breath, allowing his tantalizingly masculine blend of fragrances to fill her lungs. She loved the unique scent of him. She would be perfectly happy to stay right where she was forever. To savor the way the warmth from his large body seeped into her much smaller frame and loosened her muscles. To let her emotions continue to build until they reached a fever pitch of need. To—

"All right, I'll ask. What are you doing?" Conal's question broke into her reverie.

"Seeing if this morning was a fluke," she muttered, letting her lips brush against the taut skin on his neck.

"I certainly hope not!" His husky tone made her wonder if they were talking about the same thing.

"Maybe what I need is a distraction," she muttered. Daringly she arched her back, pushing her breasts into his chest. His reaction was immediate and very gratifying.

"I don't think I'm distracted enough." Conal grasped

her hips with his large hands and lifted her off her feet, holding her securely against his hardening manhood.

His action made her feel both helpless and exquisitely feminine. Man the conqueror. She mocked her reaction, but she still couldn't deny the desire twisting tighter and tighter through her abdomen.

"This is a bad idea," she muttered, trying to regain control of a situation that had slipped out of her grasp. Her mood had plunged from teasing good humor with sexual overtones to something violent and urgent that demanded satisfaction. A satisfaction that was impossible in her grandparents' bedroom.

"We can't do this." Her voice cracked under the weight of her frustration.

"Sure we can," Conal muttered, holding on to her with gratifying tightness.

"I know we *can*," she muttered distractedly. "I meant we *shouldn't*." Strangely enough, the fact that Conal was as affected by their closeness as she was helped her to regain a precarious grip on her seething emotions.

"Someone might come in and—"

"And find out about the birds and the bees." Conal's voice was thick with frustration. Letting go of her, he stepped back, and Livvy tried to ignore the sense of loss that engulfed her.

"And it would probably be Bobby," he added wryly. "Tell me, are all kids amateur voyeurs, or is he unique?"

Livvy giggled. "I think kids are simply more honest about their curiosity than adults. Come on. I'll introduce you to…"

Her voice trailed away as she realized that she was showing a dangerous tendency to slip into the habit of thinking of Conal as a real fiancé. This fake engagement of theirs was making it difficult for her to distinguish between what she fantasized about and what was real. And if Conal should realize that she didn't just like him, she loved him... A flush burned across her cheeks at the thought of the embarrassment it would cause. To her. It would also make him uneasy around her. Maybe even to the extent that he would want her to leave the agency. A chill of horror slipped through her at the thought.

"Why do you look so apprehensive?" Conal demanded. "What other surprise relatives have you got lurking in the bushes?"

Livvy couldn't entirely suppress a grin at his expression. "Calm down. They're all normal. Mostly," she added at his skeptical expression.

"Come on. We'll find some of my cousins to talk to."

"I'd rather go for a short walk out in that gorgeous fall weather." Conal tried to put his plan in action. To his delight, Livvy immediately agreed.

"Good idea," Livvy said, not the least bit averse to having him to herself and away from her family's curious eyes for a while. "It's turning out to be a gorgeous day." She led the way out the back door, pretending not to hear when one of her aunts called to her.

Once they'd reached the relative safety of the woods, Livvy sniffed happily at the crisp autumn air. "Doesn't it smell delicious?" she demanded.

"Different. Do you miss all this living in New York?" Conal asked, suddenly struck with the thought that perhaps she hadn't married yet because she was waiting to find a man who was willing to return to Scranton with her.

"Sure," she said. "But then I'd miss New York if I lived here all the time."

"You aren't planning to return here sometime?" Conal asked cautiously.

Livvy shook her head. "Nope, my work is in New York, and I'm close enough to visit anytime I want."

Conal relaxed slightly at her matter-of-fact words. At least that was one problem he didn't have to worry about. Now if he could just solve the rest of them. He chewed his lower lip as he tried to figure out a way to find out how she felt about children. Just blurting it out was far too blunt. She might also ask him why he wanted to know. Something he had no intention of telling her at this point.

Absently he watched a squirrel scamper up the trunk of a large maple and disappeared into the brilliant red leaves. What he needed was a casual, offhand approach. To his frustration absolutely nothing occurred to him. The problem was that asking someone whether they wanted kids wasn't a casual question. It was damned personal. In fact, some people might think it was intrusive and be offended. Would Livvy?

Uncertainly Conal shot her a glance to find her peering back through the thick tree trunks, her head cocked to one side as if she were listening to something he couldn't quite hear.

"Come on!" Grabbing his hand, she pulled him around a tree.

"What—" Conal started to ask her what she was doing, when he heard a sudden squeal and a high-pitched giggle.

"Shh," she muttered and urged him deeper into the woods.

Conal obligingly followed her, not wanting to give up their privacy to what sounded like a hoard of her young cousins.

"I think they're gone," she said, after the voices had faded into the distance. "Have a seat." She gestured toward a fallen log.

Conal gingerly sat down. "Why are you hiding from them?" he asked, hoping to use the question as a starting point to find out what he really wanted to know.

Livvy just wrinkled her nose. The endearing gesture made him want to pull her into his arms and kiss her. To slip his hands beneath her shirt and— Not now. He jerked his thoughts up short. Now he had to keep on task.

"Don't you like them?" Conal persisted.

"I like them just fine, but that doesn't mean that I want to spend all my time with them."

"Kids can be rather time consuming," Conal offered cautiously.

"Yes." Livvy flicked a black bug off the stump beside her. "They can be very expensive, too."

Conal tried to analyze her tone of voice. She'd sounded her normal, matter-of-fact self. As if she had no more than an academic interest in the disadvantages of having kids. As if she'd long ago faced those disadvantages and didn't care.

"Is that why you haven't had any?" Conal blurted out and then could have bitten his tongue at the gaucheness of the question. So much for the subtle approach, he thought in disgust.

Livvy looked up, trying to figure out the reason behind the question. Was it simply an idle one or did he have a purpose?

"I haven't had any kids because I'm hopelessly conventional." She tried to keep her response light.

Conal blinked, not understanding what she was talking about.

"No husband," Livvy elaborated at his blank look, trying to decide if this conversation was a good idea or not. Talking about children and marriage might get him thinking in those terms. Or it might make her realize that he didn't want those kinds of ties. She stifled a sigh, wishing she knew what was the best thing to say. Or do, for that matter.

"You intend to have kids once you marry?" Conal doggedly plowed on.

The tone thoroughly depressed Livvy. It sounded as if the information was of no interest to him personally. As if he could not care less what her future plans were.

"I haven't given it much thought," she muttered. Jumping to her feet she said, "We'd better get back. They'll be serving lunch before long."

Great job, Sutherland, Conal thought as he glanced at her tight features. Not only had he been unable to find out whether she wanted kids but he'd also managed to annoy her in the bargain.

Maybe he should forget about kids for the moment. He needed to concentrate on the more immediate problem of how he was going to convince her to continue their role as lovers beyond the weekend, he decided, as he trudged back to the house with her.

"Livvy," a thin young man with Livvy's dark hair and blue eyes called to her as they entered the front door. "I've been looking for you. Aunt Marie said you're engaged to some important..." He paused as he suddenly noticed Conal behind her.

"Conal, this is my cousin, Luke Farrell. Luke, my fiancé Conal Sutherland." Livvy introduced them, wondering what her mother was telling the relatives about Conal. Marie wouldn't tell an outright lie. At least, Livvy didn't think she would, but Marie wasn't above stretching the truth pretty thin to serve her own purposes.

"Pleased to meet you." Luke enthusiastically pumped Conal's hand. "Do you really run your own business?"

"Yes," Conal said cautiously.

"Great!" Luke beamed at him. "I'm thinking of buying a garage, and I wondered if you could give me a few pointers on the hazards of owning a business."

"Sure," Conal said, trying to figure out why Livvy looked so annoyed at her cousin's request.

To his relief, if Luke did have an unsocial quirk to his personality he was keeping it well hidden. He listened to what Conal had to say, asked intelligent questions that showed he'd already done a certain amount of research on the intricacies of the federal tax code and then profusely thanked Conal for his advice, saying that he was going to take the plunge and buy the business.

"All right." Conal turned to Livvy once Luke had left. "What's the matter?"

Livvy grimaced. "I was exerting all my efforts to keep from screaming."

"Why?"

"Because I gave Luke the exact same advice you just did the last time I was home, and he ignored it because I'm just a woman. You, on the other hand, are male and therefore believable."

Conal shrugged. "If Luke is stupid enough not to take advantage of your business acumen, that's his loss."

Livvy stared into Conal's serious features, and the tight knot of anger twisting her stomach eased. She still didn't like it that Luke ignored her and listened to a virtual stranger, but somehow Conal's matter-of-fact reaction helped her to put the situation into perspective. It really didn't matter what Luke thought of her business skills. What mattered was that she had them and that Conal appreciated them.

"Livvy, girl!" Her grandfather's gruff voice interrupted her thoughts, and she turned to the old man. "Quit

monopolizing the lad. Us men are going to watch Notre
Dame play Southern Cal on the television in the den.''

"And no doubt sample that rotgut you brew out in the
barn!''

"Who, me!'' Her grandfather's look of psuedo-aston-
ishment sat oddly on his whiskered face. "Don't you
know that moonshine is illegal, girl?''

"Sure, I just hadn't realized that you knew it!''

Her grandfather gave her a reproachful look and turned
to Conal. "Well, lad, you a fan of Notre Dame's?''

"He probably is, since he played line for them for four
years," Livvy said in resignation, seeing her brief time
with Conal diminishing by the length of the football game.

"What!'' Her grandfather's mouth fell open. "You actually played for Notre Dame? The real one in Indiana?''

"Yes," Conal admitted, wishing that Livvy hadn't said
anything. He hated being asked to recount stories from
his playing days. It always made him feel as if he were
some kind of freak on exhibition. Although as aggressively Irish as Livvy's family seemed to be, maybe having
played for Notre Dame would finally give him some kind
of link to the other men.

"My God.'' Her grandfather breathed the words like a
prayer. "To think the family's going to get someone who
played for Notre Dame. Livvy, I take back all the things
I ever said about you being too choosy. You done the
family proud! Wait'll I tell everyone.'' He started to turn
away and then suddenly asked, "Say, lad, you didn't happen to play pro ball after college, did you?''

"I was with the Rams for ten years," Conal admitted.

"Wow!'' Grandfather Donagher rubbed his hands together gleefully as he hurried off to spread the word.

Livvy sighed. "I don't know why I bother. Everything
I've managed to accomplish in my life, and the only thing

that means anything to my grandfather is that I'm engaged to a man who spent his Saturdays committing legalized assault.''

Conal chuckled at her aggrieved expression. "Look on the bright side. Maybe this will make them forget my suggestion last night that the men do the dishes?''

Livvy grinned back at him. "Sorry, I don't think even Notre Dame is enough to wipe out a faux pas of that size.''

"Conal, Grandpa just told us. Come and show us how to rush the passer.'' A hoard of Livvy's younger cousins erupted into the room.

Conal stared down at them. Their eager expressions gave him a strange feeling. A feeling of belonging.

"Come on, Conal!'' They grabbed his hand and began to tug him away.

"You guys return him in the same good shape you got him,'' Livvy called after them.

Eight

"I see you've found a quiet corner, my dear." Grandma Donagher collapsed into an easy chair across from Livvy with a sigh. "I dearly love all my great-grandchildren, but there's no denying that they're hard on my nerves at times. Sometimes I think that modern parents have lost sight of who's supposed to be in charge."

Livvy chuckled. "Or maybe modern parents are simply more honest about it than your generation."

Her grandmother smiled. "Maybe, but at least we knew where to draw the line. Wait till you have kids of your own. You'll see what I mean."

Chance would be a fine thing, Livvy thought glumly. She remembered Conal's odd questions about children in the woods earlier. Although maybe she was reading things into his questions that he hadn't meant. They had been hiding from her young cousins. Maybe it had simply been an idle question on his part?

Try as she might, Livvy couldn't quite believe it. Couldn't quite shake the nagging feeling that he'd had a purpose in mind. A purpose that boded no good for her future plans.

"Conal, there you are. Come here," her grandmother called.

Livvy shook herself free of her discouraging thoughts and turned to see Conal standing in the doorway. There were grass stains on the knees of his tan slacks and a dirt smudge on the front of his pale yellow shirt. She frowned as she noticed the darkening bruise on his jaw.

"What have they done to you?" Livvy demanded as he sat down on the couch beside her.

"Now, Livvy, don't fuss," her grandmother said.

Livvy ignored her as she gently ran the tips of her fingers over his discolored skin.

"Livvy, men hate fussing," Grandma Donagher repeated.

He didn't know about men in general, Conal thought, but this particular man loved it when Livvy fussed over him. It made him feel as if she really cared what happened to him. Even though he was relatively certain that her expressed concern was part of her act as his fiancée, he still found it seductive.

"What happened?" Livvy demanded.

"It was just a touch football game," Conal told her.

Livvy frowned. "Touching what? From the looks of it, what you were touching was the ground!"

Conal grinned at her. "You should have seen the rest of the team."

"Boys will be boys, dear," Grandma Donagher offered.

No, Livvy thought, Conal most emphatically was not a boy. He was a man in every sense of the word. Her eyes lingered on the firm twist of his mouth. And she could hardly wait until they got back to Fern's to reaffirm his masculinity.

"Conal, you never did tell me how many children you and Livvy were intending to have? Six is a nice round number," Grandma Donagher suggested hopefully.

"Six!"

Livvy's voice echoed the horror Conal felt. How could he have even a hope of coping with six kids? One maybe, or even two on a good day. But not six. Never six.

"And that way they can take care of you in your old age," Grandma Donagher told her.

"If I had six kids, I wouldn't live to have an old age," Livvy shot back. "I prefer my families in more manageable sizes."

"Bah! Babies are fun. Livvy was such an adorable little thing. Have you shown him any of your baby pictures, Livvy?"

"No, and I don't intend to," Livvy said.

Her grandmother beamed at her. "Then I will. Go up to the attic and bring me down that blue box that's in the top drawer of the old bureau at the head of the stairwell."

"We'd love to." Livvy hurriedly jumped to her feet. It would give her a chance to escape her grandmother's increasingly personal catechism and a few minutes alone with Conal.

"Sorry about that," Livvy said as she hustled him up to the attic before one of the men saw them and tried to get him talking about football again. "But there isn't any way to stop Grandma once she gets going. Sometimes she's even worse than Nona, and that's saying something."

Conal chuckled. "I noticed, but I am kind of curious to see what kind of baby you were."

"Pretty undistinguished. In fact, if you were to compare my real early ones, I'd probably look a lot like you. Or anyone else for that matter."

"I wouldn't know," Conal said. "I don't have any baby pictures of myself."

Livvy winced at her thoughtless comment. "I'm sorry."

"It doesn't matter," Conal said.

Was it true? Livvy wondered. Or was he just saying that because he didn't want anyone to pity him? Would she miss the hundreds of baby pictures that her family had taken of her? Yes, she decided in some surprise. Even though she didn't look at them from one year to the next, it gave her a sense of security to know that they were there. To know that someone had thought she was so special that they had taken them.

What would it be like to grow up knowing that there wasn't a single person in the whole world who thought you were the greatest thing since sliced bread? To know that the people who cared for you were only doing it because it was their job. A chill shivered through her at the soul-numbing loneliness of the idea. She wanted to throw her arms around Conal and tell him that just because his parents hadn't cared enough to make an effort to give him a home didn't mean that she didn't think he was wonderful.

"Duck your head," Livvy automatically warned him as they started up the steep attic stairs.

"Do you ever wonder about your parents?" The thought formed itself into words before she realized it, and she winced at the gaucheness of her question. She might want to know, but that didn't mean that Conal wanted to share his personal life with her. Or that she had any right to ask him.

Conal shot her an uneasy glance, wondering what was behind her question. Did his lack of family diminish him in her eyes? Or was it that she had also read about how one learned socialization in a family group? Would she only consider a husband from a so-called normal background like the one she'd grown up in? Just because he felt he might be able to learn the necessary skills, it didn't necessarily follow that she believed it. Or was willing to take that chance. He didn't know. But even if that was the case, he couldn't lie to her. Not to Livvy. No matter what the consequences, it was vitally important to him that there be honesty between them.

"Not anymore," he said. "I haven't even thought of them in years."

"Really?" Livvy said doubtfully, remembering some of the talk shows she'd seen where adopted people had vehemently stated their absolute need to know who their parents were. And those had been people from supposedly happy adoptive families. Conal hadn't even had the emotional support of an adoptive home.

"Really," Conal repeated. "I have absolutely no desire to find them. They don't have anything to do with me."

"But they're your parents," Livvy protested, not understanding how he could be so noncurious about them.

Conal yanked the string hanging from the lightbulb at the top of the stairwell as he struggled to find words to make her understand.

"What is it that makes a parent?" he finally said. "The act of giving birth? From my point of view, that doesn't cut it. Families have shared memories, and I don't have any. If I were to track down my mother, what would I say to her? Hi, Mom, how have you been for the last thirty-two years?"

"Personally I'd want to know why she left me on some doorstep!" Livvy muttered.

Conal shrugged. "When I was little, I used to dream that a nasty man had kidnapped me and left me at the orphanage and that someday my folks would find me. We'd go home and live happily ever after."

Livvy winced at the glimpse she had of the lonely little boy Conal must have been, and a blind fury filled her at the callousness of the woman who had abandoned him. How could she have done such a thing?

"Of course, once I got older and more in control of my life, I realized that my mother was probably just a woman who had found herself in a situation she couldn't handle. She'd done the only thing she felt she could do. She left me at the orphanage and got on with her life. Where did your grandmother say those pictures were?"

Livvy accepted his abrupt change of subject even though she was far from satisfied with his response. It seemed much too simple for something as complicated as having been abandoned as a child.

"In the bureau over here." Livvy walked over to it and yanked on the top drawer. It didn't budge.

"Want some help?"

"I have muscles, too," she told him, giving the drawer a hard yank. It resisted for a moment, and then the drawer suddenly came free. Livvy lost her balance and fell backward.

Conal hastily grabbed for her, managing to cushion her fall as they landed on the floor with the contents of the drawer scattered all over them.

"Perhaps I should have asked about brains," he said absently, his mind busily soaking up the sensation of her soft hips pushing into his groin. It felt fantastic. He took a deep breath, greedily sucking in the faint floral scent of her hair that was brushing his face. Her scent wasn't obvious the way some women's were. It was mostly hidden from the casual observer, rather like Livvy herself.

That's me, no brains, Livvy thought ruefully, because if I had any brains, I'd move off him. A picture frame was digging into her ribs, and she shifted slightly, feeling his muscles clench in reaction. She found his instantaneous response to her nearness irresistible. Even though she knew they were in her grandparents' attic with the door open and scads of cousins roaming about who might interrupt them at any minute, she wanted to make love to him. But if she couldn't do that, she could indulge in a couple of kisses, and then she would pick up the pictures. They would go back downstairs and allow her grandmother to terminally embarrass her.

"Good Lord." Conal reached around her and plucked a picture off her thigh. "I thought naked babies on bearskin rugs were simply a cliché."

"That's not a bearskin rug. It's a piece of dark velvet," Livvy muttered, absorbing the sensation of his chest moving as he talked. It felt fantastic and she wanted more. If it felt that good when he talked, what would it feel like if he were to laugh? She shuddered longingly at the thought, wishing she could think of an appropriate joke. Unfortunately there was nothing even vaguely funny about what she was feeling. Mindshattering, yes, funny, no.

"You were an interesting-looking baby," Conal offered.

"That's one way of putting it," Livvy said, having no illusions about her looks as an infant. She was far more interested in the present.

Turning her head slightly, the edge of her mouth brushed across his cheek. The slightly roughened skin of his jaw scraped over her much softer flesh, and she shivered.

"You are so different from me," she murmured.

Conal chuckled. "What was your first clue, Sherlock? Was it perhaps the fact that my chest is flat and muscular and yours is—" He suddenly shifted onto his side, his right arm holding her trapped while his left hand covered her right breast.

Livvy gasped as reaction tore through her. The slight pressure of his hand seemed to scorch her flesh. She could feel her breast swelling in response. Slowly she ran the tip of her tongue over her suddenly dry lips. Her eyelids felt heavy, and it was becoming increasingly difficult to keep them open. They wanted to close. To shut out the ordinary world and allow her to concentrate fully on the world of the senses.

"Squishy?" Conal's deep voice flowed enticingly along her nerves.

"I am not squishy," Livvy muttered, but not with any real conviction. She couldn't seem to work up any interest in anything except how his touch was making her feel.

"Maybe it's your clothes," he agreed.

To Livvy's shock, he slipped his hand beneath her blouse. His fingers felt hot. Burningly hot against her rib cage. She took a deep breath, shivering as his hand brushed her bare skin. His fingers were rough and callused. More like those of a man who worked with his hands than a businessman who sold the products of his mind.

A small moan escaped Livvy as his hand slowly began to inch upward, his touch tightening the desire spiraling through her. Hurry, she mentally urged him, craving the feel of him touching her.

At last his hand captured her lace-covered breast, and

Livvy desperately sucked in air in a vain attempt to slow down the reaction that ripped through her already shaky composure. She trembled as he lightly flicked her nipple with his fingernail, and it convulsed into a tight bud of need.

"Conal!" Her voice was a breathless plea for more.

"You're sidetracking my scientific inquiry," he muttered.

"Stuff your science," Livvy lost patience with the subtle approach. Twisting in his arms, she pressed herself against him from chest to groin. She wiggled slightly, trying to fit her curves more closely to his.

"I can't believe what that feels like!" Conal shifted, trapping her legs between his. His hard thighs were pressing against her much-softer ones, and she could feel his rigid manhood thrusting against her abdomen. That wasn't where she wanted to feel him, she thought foggily. She wanted to feel him deep inside her. She wanted to absorb the heat of him into the very depth of her being.

Burying her face in his neck, she nibbled slightly on his skin.

Conal half turned, knocking over something as he did so. Livvy heard the muffled thud with a total lack of interest as the thing hit the floor. The only thing she cared about was that Conal not let her go.

"You are the most enticing woman," he muttered against her mouth.

"So kiss me!" Livvy lowered her head, bridging the few inches between them. Her lips met his, and pleasure mushroomed through her. Hungrily she pressed, feeling his mouth open at her movement. Long past worrying about how he might view her aggressiveness, she shoved her tongue inside his mouth. Liquid warmth seemed to spiral through her, collecting in her abdomen and making her feel slightly frantic. Instinctively she ground her belly against his hardness, trying to find some release from the sensations rocking her.

"Livvy!" Conal moaned, and the disoriented sound of his voice fed her own sense of urgency. "I—"

"Hey, you two. Quit your fooling around up there and get back downstairs."

Livvy blinked, trying to make sense of the words echoing up the stairwell.

"She's wrong," Conal muttered. "I've never been more serious in my life."

Livvy blinked, wondering what he meant. Or for that matter if she'd even heard him correctly.

"Grandma is getting impatient, and you don't want her coming up there after you, do you?" the voice added.

Fern. Livvy finally surfaced enough to identify the intrusive voice.

"We're coming," Livvy called down, reluctantly getting to her feet. "We were just—" She glanced down at Conal, her eyes lingering on the evidence of his arousal. She completely lost track of what she'd been about to say.

Fern's giggle floated up the stairs. "I have a pretty good idea what you two were doing, which is why I volunteered to come after you instead of letting Grandma."

"You are a true diplomat, Fern." Conal slowly got to his feet and began to brush the dust from the attic floor off his grass-stained pants.

"Hey, what are sisters for? See you downstairs." Fern's footsteps disappeared down the hallway below.

Uncertain of what to say, either about the seething passion of their impromptu kiss or Fern's interruption of it, Livvy finally decided to say nothing. Instead, she began to pick up the scattered pictures, hoping her grandmother didn't intend to show all the family pictures to Conal. If she did, Livvy would never get a chance to spend some time alone with him this evening. Although she knew that sooner or later the evening would have to end. A smile curved her lips. Then they would go back to Fern's house to their own bedroom where they could close the door on the rest of the world.

Five hours later Livvy was beginning to think she'd been wrong. She felt as if she were trapped in some kind of space warp where time didn't move forward. It simply revolved in continuous loops—agonizingly slow, infinitely boring, loops. She felt that if she had to listen to one more male relative rhapsodize about the wonder of her being engaged to a man who'd actually played football for Notre Dame, she would scream. Or commit an unsportsmanlike attack on one of them.

But it was more than simply boredom at their preoccupation with football that bothered Livvy. It was a seething sense of injustice that none of her male relatives had been any more than polite to Conal until they'd found out about his having played football. All of Conal's fantastic qualities—his intelligence, his sense of fair play, his business acumen, his willingness to listen to other people's ideas, his basic niceness—hadn't meant a thing to them. He'd only gained acceptance because he'd played football. It made her furious, and yet what could she say? It seemed petty and entirely fruitless to complain that they'd accepted Conal for the wrong reasons.

By the time the party finally broke up and they had returned to Fern's, Livvy was a tightly strung bundle of nerves tied together with sexual tension.

"I get the bathroom first," Bobby yelled, scooting through the front door the minute Bill unlocked it.

"And while you're there, take a bath. You're filthy," Fern ordered.

"Ah, Mom!" Bobby stopped on the bottom step. "Dirt is clean. My science book says so."

"Not on my son. And don't dawdle. The rest of us need baths, too."

"When we move to Atlanta we'll have to look for a house with two bathrooms." Bill's purposefully bright tone dropped into the silence pathetically.

"Why don't you go for broke and get three?" Conal tried to lighten the atmosphere.

"I happen to like this house and this town," Fern snapped, two bright patches of red burned across her cheekbones.

"That's all too clear!" Bill shot back. "In fact, sometimes I think you like this damned house and town better than you do me! Good night."

Bill pushed past Bobby and stomped up the stairs. A minute later the sound of his bedroom door slamming shut shook the house.

Fern instinctively took a step after him and then stopped, her shoulders sagging dispiritedly.

"Sorry about that," Fern said.

"Hey, it's no big deal." Livvy threw her arms around her sister and gave her a hug. "Everyone looses their temper occasionally."

"Even Conal?" Fern glanced at Conal, who was standing silently behind them.

"Ha! I remember the time the computer system crashed, destroying the files for a presentation we were to give that afternoon, and I couldn't find where I'd filed the backup. You could hear him yelling two blocks away," Livvy related, trying to cheer Fern up.

"Your so-called filing system would drive a saint to distraction," Conal said, trying to help.

"Are you a saint, Uncle Conal?" Bobby peered up at him curiously.

Bobby's use of the word *uncle* sent a shaft of pleasure through Livvy. It was as if Conal really were a permanent fixture in her life.

"I thought they sacrificed all the saints?" Bobby added when no one answered him.

Sacrifice? Livvy stared at Conal, her active imagination picturing him as a sacrifice. To Eros, perhaps? She gulped at the thought of a naked Conal sprawled out on a bed waiting for her to make love to him.

"Quit stalling and go take your bath," Fern said. "It's long past your bedtime."

"Ah, Mom! It's Saturday night." Bobby trudged up the stairs.

Livvy glanced from Conal to Fern's worried face. She should stay down here and try to cheer poor Fern up. But what she wanted to do was to go with Conal up to their room. She craved physical contact with Conal. A shiver of uncertainty shook her. But what did he want? Her eyes lingered on his still features. She couldn't tell. Could her earlier comments about marriage and kids have caused him to rethink his role as her lover? Could he be afraid that she expected more from him than he was willing to give?

"Why don't you and Conal go up," Fern said. "I'll just clean up the mess we left in the kitchen."

Livvy's confused thoughts were swamped by a wave of guilt at Fern's forlorn expression. How could she be so wrapped up with her own desires when her only sister was so clearly unhappy? What kind of person was she?

One who was obsessed with Conal Sutherland, Livvy answered her own question.

"I'll help you clean up first." Livvy forced the words out when Conal didn't say anything. Perhaps he felt that her first loyalty ought to be to her sister, since both he and she knew that their engagement was a pretend one.

Maybe that's where her first loyalty ought to be, Livvy thought uneasily. But if it came down to a choice between Conal and Fern, Fern would lose every time. The knowledge added to her sense of guilt as she followed Fern out to the messy kitchen.

They managed to clean up the kitchen in forty minutes, but it was almost an hour and a half later before Fern had talked out her unhappiness about the dilemma she found herself in.

Livvy simply listened, mainly because she didn't know what to say. It seemed to her that no matter which option Fern and Bill chose, one of them was going to have to give up a lot. If there was an easy solution to their problem, she sure couldn't see it.

At last Livvy was able to escape, and she hurried upstairs, intent on joining Conal. The second floor was quiet, and Livvy paused for a moment outside her bedroom door, savoring the feeling of anticipation that shortened her breathing. She'd done her duty by her sister, and now she could seek her own pleasures with a clear conscience.

Taking a deep breath, Livvy eased open the door and slipped inside. The brilliant moonlight streaming in through the open window highlighted the shadowy mound in the bed that was Conal. Livvy paused by the door waiting for him to say something. Something that would give her a clue to how he was feeling. When he didn't, she walked over to the bed and stared down at him.

He was asleep! Livvy realized with a massive sense of

disappointment. While she'd been downstairs listening to her sister and fantasizing about what she was going to do with Conal upstairs, he'd been falling asleep. How could he?

Easily, common sense answered her own question. Simply because she was obsessed with him didn't mean that he was equally obsessed with her. In fact, she could pretty much guarantee he wasn't, or he would never have fallen asleep.

Her shoulders sagged dispiritedly. She felt as if she were trapped in a situation that both frightened and fascinated her. It was a situation that she lacked the willpower to escape from, even though she knew that if she couldn't somehow manage to get Conal to rethink his aversion to marriage she was in for a great deal of unhappiness in the future. Which was all the more reason to squeeze every last drop of pleasure out of the mess now, while she had the chance. If she couldn't make love to Conal, at least she could snuggle up to him. And he might wake up sometime during the night. Especially if she were to poke him once or twice. In her sleep of course. Feeling marginally better, she hurriedly undressed and slipped in next to Conal.

Nine

Livvy stirred restively as Bobby's intrusive voice bludgeoned her delightful dream of her and Conal on their honeymoon. She snuggled closer to Conal in a futile attempt to silence both her nephew's shrill voice and Fern's exerting him to be quiet so people could sleep. It didn't work.

Disoriented, Livvy opened her eyes to find herself looking at the enticing shadow of Conal's emerging beard. The dark growth gave him a faintly piratical air that intrigued her.

Her eye caught the bright red glow of the numbers on the digital clock, and she did some quick mental computations. There was time to do what she really wanted to do before she had to get up. Make love to Conal. But how to wake him up without appearing obvious about it. Livvy stared speculatively at his sleep-relaxed features.

She would get out of bed and use the bathroom, she

decided. She would close the bedroom door behind her with more force than necessary and hope the noise would wake him up. If it didn't, she could always slam it again and then pretend to trip and fall into bed when she came back. That should do it.

Smiling in anticipation, Livvy slipped out of bed, hurriedly pulled on her fuzzy pink robe and left, closing the door behind her with a satisfying thump. Quickly she scampered down the hall to the bathroom while it was still free.

Conal stirred at the noise and unconsciously reached for Livvy. His searching hand met emptiness, and the depth of his disappointment brought him fully awake. Where was Livvy? Why hadn't she awakened him when she'd gotten up? At least to say good morning, even if she didn't want to make love to him. A feeling of foreboding filled him.

Swinging his feet out of bed, he reached for his slacks, intent on getting dressed and finding her. He didn't want to waste a single moment of their time together.

The soft knock on the door caught him by surprise, and he hurriedly zipped up his pants before going to the door and answering it.

It was Bill. A Bill who looked as if he hadn't slept very well.

"Conal, I'm sorry to bother you, but when I saw Livvy leave I thought..." He gestured helplessly. "Oh, hell, I don't know what I thought. I just feel that if I can't talk to someone I'll go nuts and..."

Bill's unwitting confirmation that Livvy had really left depressed him. Which certainly put him in the right company, Conal thought, as he studied Bill's haggard features. Sorry as he felt for Bill, he didn't want to talk to him. He wanted to go and find Livvy. To try some ploy to entice her back into bed. But if Livvy had wanted to make love to him she would have stayed in the first place; his logic reared in his ugly head. Could it be that this was her way of telling him that their fantastic interlude was over? A shaft of pain shot through him, momentarily taking his breath away.

He took a deep lungful of air, trying to still the pain. If so, it wasn't going to work, he thought grimly. He refused to allow their relationship to return to its previous nonsexual level. He refused because...because he loved her. The shocking bit of self-realization sliced through him. His feelings for Livvy went far beyond liking or even lust. He loved her. Loved everything about her from her sharp mind to her kind manner.

So now what, he wondered in confusion. What did he do now?

"Look, if this is a bad time..." Bill said.

"No. No." Conal forced the knowledge to the back of his mind. It didn't really change anything, he tried to tell himself. He still wanted the same thing he'd wanted five minutes ago. He wanted to keep Livvy beside him, always.

"I'm just not fully awake yet," Conal added. Since he couldn't do what he really wanted to, he might as well do what good manners and common decency demanded and provide a sympathetic ear for his host. The poor guy sure looked like he could use one.

"Come in while I finish dressing." Conal stepped out of the way to let Bill come in. It only took Conal a few minutes to slip into the rest of his clothes. Following Bill downstairs, he tried hard to focus on Bill's problems and not his own.

Livvy finished brushing her hair, gave herself a quick spray of her light floral perfume and then cracked the bathroom door, peering cautiously into the hall to make sure it was empty. She didn't want to get drawn into a conversation with anyone. She wanted to get back to Conal.

The hallway was empty, and Livvy raced back to the bedroom with a feeling of satisfaction. A feeling which was immediately punctured when she glanced at the bed to see if she was going to have to slam the door to wake up Conal. It was empty. Her eyes instinctively swung around the small bedroom looking for him. It too was empty. A feeling of massive disappointment crushed her thoughts, bringing them to a standstill.

Livvy sagged back against the door and stared blankly at the bed. Where could he have gone? She hadn't been gone that long. No more than five minutes, max. Was it possible that he'd been awake before she'd actually left? Could he have taken advantage of her leaving to escape before she could come back and…and what? She mocked her fears. Force him to make love to her. Conal was a grown man and perfectly capable of saying no. The same way she was. Theoretically, at least. She sighed. She didn't think she would ever be able to look at him and say no.

Although they were due to leave Scranton right after church this morning, she considered the fact. Maybe Conal had decided that it was time to return their relationship to its normal, even keel. Its normal, nonsexual even keel. She grimaced. She didn't know about him but she knew she would never be able to recapture the mental equilibrium she'd had before this weekend. And she didn't want to, she admitted truthfully. No matter what the future price might be, she couldn't regret being Conal's lover. Livvy had found a depth of response in herself that she'd never even realized she was capable of feeling. For the first time she felt complete as a woman, and she couldn't regret that.

Besides, Livvy thought, trying to rally herself. *You don't know that he left to try to let you down easy.* She struggled to come up with other reasons. But just because she couldn't think of any didn't mean that there weren't any, she reminded herself. Becoming paranoid wouldn't help the situation any. She needed to keep a clear head.

"Rome wasn't built in a day," she muttered, and then winced when she realized that she was descending to platitudes in an effort to comfort herself. What this situation called for was action. She would get dressed, go downstairs and ignore the fact that Conal had skipped out on her the minute he'd had a chance.

Determinedly she started to get dressed. Since Conal didn't know how much she'd been looking forward to making love to him, he wouldn't realize what a disappointment his leaving was to her. She tried to focus on the only saving grace she could see in the situation. She could face him with something like her normal manner. She hoped.

"Let's go for a walk while we talk," Bill said. "There's no place in the house we can speak privately."

"Fine with me." Conal stole a quick glance into the kitchen as he passed through the hall to see if Livvy was there. She wasn't, and Conal felt a twinge of disappointment that he couldn't at least see her. Just look at her and perhaps bask in the smile she always gave him. Or maybe— He yanked his imagination up short as Bill opened the front door. Bill, he reminded himself. He had promised to listen to Bill.

"I don't know what the hell to do," Bill finally said

when they reached the corner. "I really love Fern, and I want her to be happy but…"

"But you'd like to be happy, too?" Conal offered, when the silence stretched on for a half a block.

"When you say it out loud it sounds kind of selfish, doesn't it?" Bill muttered. "It's just that sometimes I think that if I have to spend one more day staring at yet another set of numbers…"

Conal shot him a curious glance, realizing he had no idea what Bill did for a living. All Livvy had said was that he worked for a local division of a large company. "Exactly what is it you do?"

"Accounting. I sit in a gray cubicle by myself and stare at a computer screen all day long. I hate it."

"You don't like accounting?"

"No, accounting I like just fine. It's the isolation I hate. The mind-numbing, repetitiveness of the job. Sometimes I get an urge to juggle the figures just to create a little excitement."

A rueful smile tugged at Conal's lips. "I wouldn't recommend it. You might get more excitement than you can handle."

"Probably, since I can't seem to handle anything else." Bill sighed. "That's why this promotion is such a godsend. It's in management. I'd have people I could interact with all day. Not only that, but it would be different. Something new. A real challenge. I just can't seem to make Fern understand."

Wanting to help, Conal searched for some useful advice and drew a blank. His understanding of the female mind was scanty. And if Bill, who'd been married to Fern for years, didn't know what to say to her, he was probably being presumptuous to think he could come up with a quick answer. Conal idly watched a squirrel scampering on the power lines overhead as he considered the situation. If he didn't know how to solve the problem by changing Fern's mind maybe he could reach the solution through Bill.

"Have you considered going to work for someone else here in Scanton?" Conal asked.

"Yes, with absolutely no success," Bill said. "The problem is that there aren't all that many jobs like mine in town. And almost none that pay as well."

So much for the easy answer, Conal thought, refusing to give up. Not only did he like Bill as a person, but Livvy would also be pleased if he were to somehow come up with an answer to the problem. Maybe pleased enough to throw her arms around him and give him a hug.

Bill! Conal hastily corralled his wandering thoughts. First accomplish the task and then contemplate the rewards.

"What would you do if you didn't have to consider anything else?" Conal asked, remembering the process he'd used to decide on a career in advertising.

Bill shot him a puzzled glance. "What do you mean?"

"If you didn't have to worry about earning a steady income or what Fern wants, what would you do?"

"Oh, that's easy," Bill said. "I'd open my own accounting agency."

"Is there a market for the service in the area?"

Bill snorted. "Judging by the number of people who are after me every spring to do their tax returns I'd say so. Actually, I played with the idea about a year ago when I started finding it such a struggle to get out of bed every morning."

"And?" Conal asked encouragingly.

Bill shrugged. "Working for yourself is a big risk. At

least with the company, I can be sure of getting a steady income."

"And hospitalization when you finally crack under the strain," Conal retorted.

Bill's shoulders sagged. "Yeah," he muttered.

"What kind of initial investment would it take to set you up in business?"

"Well, I guess I could run the business out of our house until I was making enough to rent an office downtown. I already own the computer and all the specialized software. I guess I'd just need a copier, a fax machine and some office supplies. It wouldn't take a lot of initial outlay," Bill conceded.

"So basically all you'd have to worry about is your day-to-day living expenses," Conal concluded.

"Yeah," Bill agreed, "and they aren't really that heavy. We own the house outright, and we don't owe anybody anything. Fern thinks like I do financially. If we can't afford to pay cash for something, we try to do without it."

"And Fern has a steady income," Conal added.

"Yes," Bill's voice sounded faintly more confident. "She does. She also has health insurance at her job. But when I mentioned the idea to her last year, she shot it down in flames."

"How hard did you try to convince her?"

"Not very," Bill said slowly. "To be honest, the thought of going it on my own scared me. It still does, but not as much as the thought of having to spend the rest of my life sitting in my tiny cubicle staring at a computer screen. Starting my own business was something I thought I'd like to do when everything was perfect."

"There is no time when everything is perfect," Conal

said bluntly. "All you can do is grab the moment and make the best of it."

Bill stopped and stared blankly down at the cracked concrete sidewalk in front of him for a few seconds. Finally he turned to Conal.

"You know, Conal, you could be right. And I was right, too. Talking to you was exactly what I needed to do to bring it all together in my mind. Let's go back. I want to tell to Fern about all this." He turned around and headed back to the house with a good deal more vigor in his step.

Conal's sense of pleasure was only marginally less than Bill's. Not that Conal deluded himself into thinking that he'd solved Bill's problem. Bill had known the solution all the time. He simply had needed someone to listen to him and agree with him. To validate his opinion. What made Conal so optimistic was the fact that he had been able to logically look at the seeming impasse between Bill and Fern and follow it through to a satisfactory conclusion. It made no difference to him that Bill had already traveled the route. In fact, it made it better, because that meant that he had the same problem-solving skills as a man from a so-called normal family background. A man who'd been married for years. Impersonal problem solving skills he'd learned over the years had been sufficient to solve an emotional problem.

For the first time he began to really believe and not just hope that not growing up in a normal family wasn't an insurmountable barrier to a successful marriage. Other things could be substituted. And one should never underestimate desire, he thought, reminding himself of an old adage from his football-playing days. Wanting to succeed at something gave one a huge edge in any situation. And Conal wanted to succeed with Livvy more than he'd ever wanted anything in his life. The very thought of getting to marry her and going home with her every night was incentive enough to change the world, not just himself.

But his self-confidence dipped a little when he remembered Bobby's scornful stare. Did kids respond to logic, too? But kids didn't start out as six-year-olds. They started out as babies. Babies who wouldn't have any preconceived expectations of what a father should be. A baby would take him as he found him. He would have time to get some firsthand experience at parenting before he had to worry about anything more challenging than feeding and changing it.

And Livvy knew all about kids. His spirits began to rise. She'd grown up in a normal family. He grimaced as he remembered her elderly great-uncles. Livvy had grown up in a relatively normal family, he thought. She would know how to go about raising a kid. She would help him.

Always provided he could somehow manage to convince her that she wanted to marry him in the first place. Conal refused to dwell on it, because having a thought of failure predisposed one to fail—he dredged up yet one more platitude from his playing days.

Conal hurried along beside Bill, eager to get the morning over with so that he and Livvy could get back to New York and among familiar surroundings. Surroundings that would hopefully give him some ideas on how to accomplish his goal.

Livvy absently took another sip of her coffee and tried to think. In two hours they would be on their way home and then what? Where would their relationship be? She didn't know. Where did she want it to be? She tried to attack the problem from another angle. Her mind instantly pictured her standing at the altar, but instead of a priest intoning the sacred words of the marriage sacrament, she kept hearing Conal saying that Fern should give up her job and move to Atlanta with Bill. As if everything Fern had accomplished counted for nothing besides Bill's career needs.

Uncertainly Livvy stared into the steaming depths of her coffee. Was that the way Conal thought about wives in general or in just this case? She didn't know. Nor was it relevant at the moment, she tried to tell herself. At the moment her primary concern was how to get him to continue their relationship once they were back home. First, she'd worry about extending their short-term relationship. Because if she didn't she'd never get the chance to worry about long-term problems that might crop up.

Right, she nodded her head emphatically, feeling slightly relieved to only have to worry about one thing at a time. So how could she do it? Maybe when they got back to New York she could invite Conal in for a cup of coffee. She could say that they should discuss what they were going to do about those political TV spots that the congresswoman wanted. And since they really did need to discuss it sometime, he probably wouldn't think that she had an ulterior motive.

Her spirits rose fractionally. If she were lucky, she'd have him seduced before he realized that he was wrong. So how did one seduce a man like Conal?

She'd think of something, Livvy encouraged herself as she started to pack. Desperation would give her an idea, because if she didn't come up with a way to seduce him she might never get another chance. They'd go back to their normal routine at the office and, while they were together for long periods of time each day, you could hardly make love to someone in the office, could you? She fell into a delightful revelry as she considered what could be accomplished in her supply closet.

Ten

Livvy waved one last time at her sister as Conal pulled away from the curb and then sagged back in her seat, feeling drained.

"Tired?" Conal asked.

"Not exactly. A visit to my family always leaves me feeling a little like a limp dishrag. And this one—"

"Was worse?" Conal tried to keep the tension out of his voice.

Livvy looked up, hearing his tone. He didn't think she meant because he'd been there, did he? She rushed to explain.

"Yes, it's very uncomfortable to be a guest when one's hosts are fighting. And then to have Fern go off the deep end about the advice you gave Bobby! Honestly, you'd think you'd given the kid a loaded gun and sent him out with instructions to shoot to kill."

"You don't agree with your sister's views on nonviolence?" Conal asked, heartened by her indignant tone.

"In the abstract I do, but let's face it, life's more than an abstraction. Fern's policy of ignoring the problem sure wasn't working."

Conal felt some of his tenseness dissipate. Livvy seemed to be far closer to his ideas of how to raise a child than her sister's. But then Livvy was a very practical person. She didn't spend her time lamenting what wasn't; she dealt with what was. Was she practical enough to see the advantages of being married to him? Was she practical enough to see what a great team they would make? Or would her practicality make her leery of taking a risk on him?

"Although," Livvy continued, "I don't think that Fern would have reacted quite so strongly if she hadn't already been on edge about Bill's wanting to move to Atlanta. Poor Fern."

"I talked to Bill this morning." Conal deftly edged the car into the right lane. "And he has an idea about opening his own accounting firm."

"Which would mean they wouldn't have to leave." Livvy immediately saw the benefits. She stared speculatively at Conal. "Opening his own business sounds a lot more like you than Bill. He brings whole new shades of meaning to the term *cautious*. Did you suggest it?"

"No, it was his idea. I think he's more afraid of being stuck in the same job for the rest of his life than he is of failing."

"No reason the business should. He's good at his job, and related to half the town. If the family *alone* goes to him, he'll be a success," she said, feeling much better now that she knew that Fern's problem had been solved. That only left her to worry about why Conal had sided with Bill. And what future implications that might have for her.

Livvy scrambled around in her mind, trying out and discarding several oblique questions as being simply too oblique. Just ask him, she told herself.

"Conal," she said slowly, "why did you think that Fern should be the one to make the sacrifice and not Bill?"

Conal took his eyes off the road long enough to give her a quick glance, wondering what was behind the question. He wasn't sure. But ducking her question wouldn't be smart, of that he was sure.

"Because, even though Fern would have to start over, she could still teach and she loves teaching. Bill on the other hand hates what he's doing now."

"I see," Livvy said slowly, as she considered his explanation. It wasn't the conclusion she had reached, but it was reasonable and based on the facts as he saw them. And, far more importantly, his decision hadn't been based on the fact that Fern was the wife and thus should give way. Her initial reading of Conal's view of women in the workplace had been correct.

Which was a good thing, because she simply didn't have the strength to walk away from him. To never see him again. A sluggish feeling of icy fear trickled through her mind. To never argue with him about the best way to present the idea the client was aiming for. To never spend half the night putting the last-minute touches on a project. To never laugh with him over some of the foibles of their clients.

On some basic level Conal was necessary to her mental well-being. To say nothing of her emotional well-being.

She looked over at Conal, her eyes lingering on the strength of his large hands as they grasped the steering wheel. An unsought prickle of awareness danced over her skin at the memory of his fingers touching her.

Livvy bit her lip, using the pain as a focus to pull herself free of her erotic thoughts. This wasn't the time to wallow in a sexual fantasy. This was the time to plan. To decide exactly what she was going to do once she got back to her apartment.

A lot depended on what Conal did. Would he continue to treat her as a lover? A surge of excitement made her shift restlessly, and the sunlight caught the engagement ring she'd forgotten she was wearing.

Why hadn't Conal asked for it back when they'd left Fern's? It was a very valuable diamond.

Livvy rubbed her forehead, which was beginning to ache from the strain of trying to answer so many unanswerable questions.

"Headache?" Conal's voice caught her by surprise. She had thought that he was totally focused on the heavy traffic.

"Tension," she gave him the absolute truth.

"Why don't you take a nap," he said. "We need to decide what we're going to do about those spots for the congresswoman, when we get back to New York."

Livvy felt as if Conal were reading his lines from the script she'd written. Of course, how long that lasted was anybody's guess. Which was all the more reason to take the maximum advantage of it while things were going her way. She closed her eyes to think, but promptly drifted off to sleep.

Conal glanced down at Livvy's sleep-relaxed face and felt a sudden twist of tenderness. He wanted to carry her back to his apartment instead of her own. He wanted to take her in his arms and make passionate love to her. To seal the two of them up in their own little world. It seemed an act of cruelty that he should be separated from her after the weekend they'd just shared.

Making love to her had been the defining point of his life. Everything else paled beside it. And if he didn't get to do it again... His fingers tightened on the steering wheel in negation of the idea. He would. Because if he didn't... He swallowed, refusing to focus on worst-case scenarios. He needed to hold a positive thought if he were going to pull this off.

If only he knew precisely how she felt about him. A flush skated over his cheekbones as he thought about how she felt to him. Warm and soft and supple and inviting. He hurriedly pulled his imagination up short as the car shot forward in response to his foot's unconsciously increased pressure on the gas pedal.

After they'd decided what they were going to do about the congresswoman's offer, he would try to kiss Livvy and, if she didn't slap him down, he would try to make love to her. That would be enough to keep him going until he could figure out some way to convince her that he was a good risk for marriage.

A car suddenly cut in front of him, and Conal forced himself to focus on the traffic. Winding up in traction was definitely not going to advance his cause.

"Wake up, Livvy," Conal said, once he'd parked the car in her apartment house's basement garage.

His words slipped into her dreams, adding an erotic tint. Livvy smiled, instantly recognizing the deep tones. Blindly she reached for Conal, her arms closing around his shoulders. She tugged him toward her, feeling a hot, melting warmth drop through her as his firm lips met hers. She twisted slightly, trying to pull him closer.

Something hard jabbed into her ribs, and she muttered,

protesting against his lips. Livvy prised her eyelids open and found herself staring into Conal's bright eyes.

Not a dream! A flush of embarrassment shook her. Hastily she sat up, managing to bump her forehead against his chin in the process.

"Sorry," she muttered, scrambling to wake up.

"Leave the luggage for now," Conal said as she fumbled ineffectively with the car door handle. "I'll bring them up later, after we decide what we want to do about that campaign for the congresswoman."

Later? Livvy thought. That sounded as if he intended to spend the whole evening with her. Her spirits rose.

Livvy hurried across the garage and into the elevator, her mind busily considering and then disregarding various ploys of seduction. Most of the methods she'd seen used in the movies had depended on either exotic lingerie or dangerous situations. Unfortunately, even though she had an appropriate outfit, she couldn't think of a single casual way to change into it.

And the only danger she was in was that she was likely to lose her mind from extreme frustration, which probably didn't count.

Livvy still hadn't managed to figure out a way to accomplish her goal when she unlocked her apartment door. Pushing it open, she stepped inside and allowed its quiet peace to flow soothingly over her agitated nerves.

Conal followed her inside, wondering where the bedroom was. He glanced toward a half-open door leading off the kitchen. In there?

Livvy noticed his interest, and a sudden surge of panic evaporated the last lingering dregs of sleep clouding her mind. Her paintings were in that room. She couldn't let him see them. It would undoubtedly push their relationship to a crisis point, and she wasn't ready for that yet. Not anywhere nearly ready.

Trying to appear casual, she walked over and closed the door to her study. To her relief, Conal didn't comment.

"Have a seat while I put some coffee on," Livvy said, using the familiar routine of making coffee to try to calm her jittery nerves. It helped somewhat. By the time the coffee was brewed, she felt a little more like her normal self.

Livvy sat down on the couch, surreptitiously studying Conal who was scribbling on his notepad. There were faint lines of concentration wrinkling his forehead. He looked so adorable. She wanted to soothe out those wrinkles with her lips.

"This actually looks promising," he finally said.

Promising? Livvy examined his choice of words and dismissed it out of hand. *Promising* didn't begin to describe what kissing him was like. *Euphoric* maybe or...

"Livvy? Are you still asleep?"

He wasn't talking about kissing. She made a valiant effort to redirect her wayward thoughts.

"Sorry," she muttered, "you were saying?"

"That doing the congresswoman's spots will bring us to the attention of all kinds of potential clients."

Livvy grimaced. "Probably. There does seem to be a plethora of politicians littering the landscape these days."

"You're letting your prejudices interfere with your business sense."

"It's not my prejudices that are bothering me. It's my principles!"

"If you don't like the way political advertising has gone—"

"Down the toilet," she muttered, but he ignored her.

"Then this is your chance to make a difference."

"Have you forgotten the soup campaign?"

"No, and you'd better not, either. I'm not asking you to do this one. Just to share a few ideas with me on what direction you think we should take." He stared at the wall, thinking for a long moment, and then he said, "Maybe we ought to add another person to the office."

Livvy felt her spirits sink. She didn't want another person in the office. Another person tying up Conal's time. Intruding on their work sessions.

"Why don't you worry about that if and when we get the soup campaign," she said, trying to postpone the inevitable. To her relief, he nodded.

"How do you think political campaigns should be run?" Conal asked.

"On issues, revolutionary as it might sound!" she said tartly. "I would like to see a commercial tell me where the candidate stands on an issue."

"As opposed to where her opponent stands?" Conal asked thoughtfully.

"I guess," Livvy said slowly. "But it seems to me that we're getting into a murky area there."

"Life's full of murky areas." Conal tossed his notebook on the coffee table.

If only he knew, Livvy thought. Her whole life seemed to be a gray area lately.

"Spare me the pop psychology and drink your coffee," she said, not wanting to think about her own uncertainties.

"I want some cream for it," he said, fearing her order was a prelude to her telling him to go home.

Livvy's dark eyebrows rose. "Since when do you drink cream in your coffee?"

"Since now."

"I haven't got any cream."

"Then I'll take milk," he said. "Your uncle Harry said that drinking milk in your coffee negates the effect of the caffeine."

"Uncle Harry also says that a shot of whiskey first thing in the morning and last thing at night is the secret to longevity!"

A sudden smile quirked Conal's lips, and Livvy felt a feeling of tenderness flow through her partially dissolving her fears.

"Does this mean I can't have any milk?" he asked.

"No, it doesn't mean that." Getting to her feet, she went into her tiny kitchen. It was while she was pouring some milk into the creamer that she suddenly had a brilliant flash of inspiration. She filled the creamer to the brim, sent up a silent prayer for whatever saint was in charge of lost causes and went back to Conal.

Carefully timing her action, she walked toward him. When she was almost there, she pretended to trip, and carefully flung the milk all over him. She watched in satisfaction as the white liquid soaked into his shirt and ran down his pants, leaving dark, wet lines.

"Oh, dear, I'm so sorry!" She put every ounce of acting ability she had into the apology. "I guess I'm still a little off balance from that nap on the way home."

Conal winced as a stray drop of the cold milk trickled over his groin. He looked into her eyes, and his discomfort was forgotten at the seething emotion he could see in her bright blue eyes. Could she have done that on purpose to get him out of his clothes? The thought made him lightheaded for a moment before common sense intervened. The emotion he could see in her eyes was probably nothing more than embarrassment.

"I hate the smell of sour milk," he offered tentatively.

"I'm so sorry," Livvy repeated. "The least I can do is to wash your clothes for you before the milk sets."

And what would be the most she could do for him? he wondered. Excitement slammed through him at the obvious answer.

"Thanks," he mumbled, finding it harder and harder to act naturally. "I'll take these off so you can put them in the washer." He looked around, and seeing the hallway off the living room, realized that it probably led to her bedroom. He could change in there. His breathing shortened at the thought of what else he could do in there.

"Be back in minute," he muttered, trying his best to keep his rising excitement from her attention.

Livvy watched the supple movement of his hips as he walked toward the bedroom. He had the most fascinating musculature, she thought dreamily. She could spend hours exploring the exact feel and texture of each individual muscle. At least, she could if she could somehow force herself to wait. Somehow she always seemed to get caught up in a sense of urgency the minute she felt his naked body up against hers, and feeling his muscles became secondary to feeling him inside her.

Livvy froze. Naked body? Conal's naked body? A life-sized painting of what she'd imagined his naked body would look like was hanging on her bedroom wall! He would see it!

The horrific thought sent her sprinting after him, madly praying that he hadn't noticed it yet. She burst into her bedroom to find Conal removing his pants. Startled, he turned toward her, and for a moment she forgot what she was worried about at the sight of his magnificent body. She gulped as her eyes lingered on the evidence of his state of mind. A twisting sensation gripped her abdomen, and it was all she could do not to fling herself into his arms.

"I would have brought them out to you," he said, and the husky timber of his voice reminded her why she'd followed him.

Carefully avoiding looking at the picture, she forced herself to focus on his face. His features seemed tauter, in sharper relief than they had been. As if he were under pressure. Lots of pressure. Maybe he hadn't noticed the picture, she hoped. Plenty of people never looked at the pictures on the wall.

Drawn by the lure of his powerful body, Livvy crossed the room and accepted the damp clothes he was holding.

"I was looking for something to wrap around myself," he offered, thrown off balance by both her sudden appearance and the astonishing painting of him on the wall. He wanted to know what it meant. He knew what he wanted it to mean—that she was one-tenth as fascinated by him as he was by her. But how could he find out? How did one casually ask someone why they had a nude painting of you hanging on their wall? His mind couldn't come up with a single, plausible idea.

Livvy shifted the bundle of clothes from one hand to the other, unable to take her eyes off the way his powerful chest moved with his every breath. Do something, she urged herself. Let him know that you want to make love to him. Just be careful to phrase it casually, so that if he turns you down... Her mind shied away from the thought of dealing with the pain and embarrassment of a rejection. But daunting as that thought was, the thought of not getting to make love with him was even worse.

Taking a deep breath, Livvy tentatively put her hand out and ran her fingertips over the line of his collarbone.

Her intense nervousness eased a little as he shivered violently in reaction.

"What are you doing?" Conal's voice seemed to echo strangely in her ears.

"I'm trying to figure out a way to casually ask you if you want to make love to me." The words spilled out. Her eyes widened, unable to believe she'd actually said that.

"Yes," he said tightly and, grabbing his clothes out of her unresisting hands flung them away before he yanked her up against him.

Tension of another sort began to spiral through her, tightening her muscles and fogging her mind. Dreamily she raised her head and found herself staring into the painting of Conal. A feeling of panic was added to the confusing mixture of emotions running through her. If they stayed here for any length of time, it was inevitable that he would notice the picture. And Conal being Conal, he wouldn't wonder in silence. He would ask and that would lead to all kinds of questions she would rather not deal with.

"Um, Conal?"

"What?" His breath warmed her neck, sending a series of shivers coursing over her.

"I always wanted to make love under the covers. Like in a tent. You know, kind of the sheik of Araby thing?" She blurted out the first idea that came to mind.

"I'll trade you your fantasy for mine." He nibbled lightly on the throbbing vein in her neck.

Livvy tilted her head back, the better to allow him access, and muttered, "What fantasy?"

"When I bought my apartment, the salesman said that the Jacuzzi was the perfect size to make love to someone in, and I've always wanted to try it."

Livvy felt a surge of happiness at his words. Not only had he never made love to anyone in his Jacuzzi but he was also obviously intending on extending their affair.

Being careful to keep her body between him and the painting, Livvy urged him toward her bed and pulled up the peach-colored silk comforter. "Climb under," she urged, breathing a sigh of relief when he promptly did as she told him to.

Livvy quickly stripped off her clothes with more haste than finesse and scrambled in after him.

It was dark under the comforter and she blinked, trying to see. Not that she really needed to. Conal would be impossible to lose in this small a space. The heat pouring off his body was like a neon sign flashing in the darkness, signaling his whereabouts.

Reaching out, she encountered his upper arm. She rubbed her fingertips over his supple skin, shivering convulsively as his biceps contracted. Livvy gulped, feeling as if the bottom had dropped out of her stomach. She loved the way he felt. She loved the way he made her feel. As if she were the most feminine woman in the world. But not passively feminine. Aggressively feminine. Totally in control of what was going on.

Her fingers inched across his shoulder and down over his broad chest, encountering one of his flat nipples. Momentarily distracted, she examined it, smiling happily when he jerked. She felt hot. Hot and pliable. Plastic, as if she could mold herself into anything he wanted a lover to be.

"You have the most intriguing vestigial remains," she announced.

"You on the other hand talk too much." Conal's arm suddenly slipped beneath her slim body, and he jerked her toward him. Livvy landed up against him with mind-blowing force. In every place she was touching him, her nerves sparked to instant life. Clamoring for satisfaction.

Conal's long fingers speared through her tousled hair, and he cupped her head, tilting her face toward him. Livvy could sense him coming closer in the darkness.

She wiggled slightly, gasping as her thigh bumped against the turgid hardness of him. Her lips parted and she dragged in air to her suddenly constricted lungs.

She could feel his breath on her cheek, and she blindly turned toward the promise of closer contact. Unerringly his mouth closed over hers, insistently pressing. Eagerly her lips parted and he pushed his tongue inside, bringing a burning sweetness with it.

Livvy moaned deep in her throat as he took his time to explore her mouth. His tongue slid enticingly over hers and she frantically gripped his head, holding him tightly against her.

She wanted him now. She wanted to feel the heavy weight of his body pressing her into the mattress. She wanted to feel his manhood deep within her, making her feel cherished. She wanted to experience the mind-blowing sensation of having him move in her.

Frantically she tugged at his broad shoulders, trying to pull him on top of her. She might as well have been pulling on an oak tree for all the difference it made.

Conal's lips left her mouth and began to nuzzle the soft skin behind her ear. "You smell so fantastic." His deep, vibrant voice seeped into her flesh, heightening her sense of urgency. "And you taste even better." His tongue flicked out, and he flicked her earlobe.

Livvy jerked as a hot shard of emotion jabbed her. She felt as if she'd been burned. Branded by his mouth.

"Conal," she whispered urgently. "Please make love to me."

"I thought I was." He lightly bit her earlobe, and when she moaned, he took it into his mouth and pulled on it gently.

The texture of his mouth excited her nerve endings, and Livvy gulped, trying to swallow, but her mouth was too dry. She felt as if she were on fire. Burning up with the force of her desire for Conal.

It's the heat from being under the comforter, she told herself, trying to grasp at a rational explanation for the irrational feelings tearing her apart. Then all semblance of rationality fled as his hands moved slowly down over her body. She could feel the faint tremor in his fingers as he touched her breasts and trailed down over her quivering stomach. It was a tremor that was echoed deep within her.

"I need," she began, and the words escaped on a sudden whoosh of air as his hand slipped between her legs to probe the moistness there.

"I can feel what you need," he grated out. "It's what I need, too."

With a supple movement, he slipped between her legs and carefully positioned himself. Livvy grabbed ineffectively at his hips, trying to force him to hurry. To hurry before she lost her mind.

"You are so delicate," he muttered. "So very delicate." He pushed forward in one smooth movement, and Livvy gasped.

Resting his arms on either side of her body, he raised his body slightly and moved forward. His hardness seemed to push against the very core of who and what she was. The exquisite sensation was too much for her to contain. Too much to try to hold in check, but she tried. Tried to prolong the sensations ripping her apart.

Back and forth he moved, while Livvy flung her head back and concentrated on the exaltation which threatened to swamp her. Finally her control snapped, and she was hurled into a world of such pure sensation that the beauty of it sent tears trickling down her face. Dimly she was aware of Conal's muffled shout of release, but it didn't really have any meaning for her. Nothing had any meaning at that precise moment but her own feelings.

She finally surfaced enough to realize that Conal had fallen asleep. His deep peaceful breathing was the perfect counterpoint to his earlier pleasure.

Cautiously she counted to a hundred. When he didn't wake up, she slowly crawled out of bed and stealthily crept across the bedroom to the painting. In a few minutes she'd taken it down and stashed it in the back of her closet.

She let out a long satisfied sigh and headed back to the bed. Somehow, against the odds, she'd managed to keep him from noticing it. Maybe her luck was a sign of the future, and fortune intended to keep smiling on her. Superstitiously she crossed her fingers as she slipped back beneath the covers and snuggled up to the comforting warmth of Conal's large body.

"Mr. Sutherland, as your lawyer I would be derelict in my duty if I didn't tell you that this is a very bad idea. All you have to do is look around you to know that marriages don't last. You've worked very hard to build up all this." John Malloy waved his hand around Conal's cluttered office. "What are you going to do if that happens to you? Ask—" he glanced down at the name on the document he'd prepared for Conal "—this Olivia Farrell to please give back the half of the company you gave her as a wedding present?"

"My marriage isn't going to fail." Conal accepted the folder John Malloy reluctantly handed him.

The lawyer snorted derisively. "If I had a dollar for every love-sick fool who told me that—"

"I'm not a fool, lovesick or otherwise." Conal cut him off, getting tired of the man's gloomy predictions. They were too close to his own half-formed fears for him to be able to dismiss them out of hand. Not that he was so much afraid that Livvy would divorce him as he was that she would refuse to marry him in the first place.

Giving her half the agency was the only idea he had come up with to show her that he was serious about working at marriage. That he was committed to making theirs a success.

Conal deliberately tried to focus on the three things that had kept him hoping, during this interminable past week since they'd returned from Scranton. That incredible painting of him she had in her bedroom, which had mysteriously disappeared after they'd made love. Also, she hadn't returned his ring, even though she wasn't wearing it in the office, and she had made no attempt to shut him out of her personal life.

Malloy shook his head in exasperation. "Well, I tried."

Conal shook hands with Malloy and waited until the lawyer had left his office before he sat back down and stared at the cream folder in the center of his desk. Two sheets of paper. Such a thin document to be pinning so much hope on.

Conal leaned back and stared blindly at the ceiling as he tried to get his jumpy nerves under control with deep breathing. It didn't help. Deciding that if he didn't ask her soon, he wasn't going to be in any kind of shape to ask her at all, he got to his feet and headed to her office. He wanted to know her answer. He couldn't stand the stomach churning uncertainty that had tormented him for the past week.

Livvy looked up as her office door opened to reveal Conal. Her breath caught in her throat, and a wave of intense longing shot through her at the sight of his beloved face.

A jolt of nervousness heavily laced with fear shot through Conal as he looked at her, and he was suddenly overwhelmed with last-minute doubts. Maybe this wasn't the best time to ask her? Maybe he ought to wait. He realized, though, that she wasn't any more likely to accept him later.

Taking a deep breath, he opened his mouth to recite the proposal he'd practiced last night. Nothing came out. His mind was a complete blank.

He gulped and scrambled frantically through his confused thoughts, looking for something, anything, to say.

Livvy eyed him in sudden fear. He looked upset. Ill at ease. As if he were trying to think of a way to tell her that he was tired of playing the part of her lover. That he wanted her to return his ring. Maybe he had expected her to return it once they got back without him having to ask.

Livvy tensed her muscles. She didn't dare let him know how much a rejection would hurt her. As long as she kept it casual she could continue to work with him. Continue to see him on a day-to-day basis, and while it would be like having to subsist on bread and water after having feasted on caviar, it was a lot better than nothing. Which was what she'd have if she had to leave.

"I..." Conal struggled to force the words out. "M-marry me!" erupted a second later seemingly of its own accord. He heard his unadorned words echo around the room in horror. He wanted to grab them back. To embellish them with heartfelt promises and logical reasons why she should.

"Marry me, and I'll give you half the agency." He

shoved the papers at her and then almost groaned at the mercenary sound of his words. How could he be screwing this up so badly when he'd practiced so hard?

Livvy simply stared at him, hearing the fateful words echoing in her ears. She'd wanted to hear them for so long she was almost afraid to believe that she really had. Afraid it was some kind of hallucination.

"I know I'm not a good risk as a husband," he muttered, "but—"

Livvy blinked, taken aback by his words. She swallowed and tried to think rationally. She couldn't seem to get past Conal's asking her to marry him.

"I mean…I know that I don't have any experience at how families operate," he continued doggedly.

"From where I'm standing that's a definite plus," she said wryly.

Conal looked into her beloved face and felt a slight easing of the tension that was strangling him.

"I'm willing to do anything I can to make our marriage a success," he offered, "and that's why I'm willing to give you half the agency. So you'll know I'm totally committed to it."

A *success*, she weighed the word, having no trouble believing that Conal would devote his whole heart to the goal. He was a very single-minded kind of person.

But what had made him propose? The question nagged at her. He'd always been so adamantly against marriage. Although come to think of it, he hadn't said anything that could be interpreted as antimarriage since they'd returned from Scranton.

"Why marriage?" she decided to simply ask.

"Because I love you! Why the hell do you think?" The words seemed to explode from him.

They enveloped Livvy, wrapping her in a sense of euphoria. Conal loved her! The words sang in her mind as if they were a symphony. Conal loved her.

"I don't want half the business," she said.

Conal stared down at her, his heart beating so hard that it felt as if it was trying to climb up his throat. "Is that a yes or a—" He couldn't bring himself to say the word.

"Yes," Livvy said, and felt a sense of peace, of rightness steal through her. "I love you to distraction, Conal Sutherland."

Conal grabbed her, crushing her up against him. His mouth covered hers with an urgency that Livvy found intoxicating. Every fear for the future she'd ever had paled to insignificance next to the knowledge that Conal loved her. There was nothing they wouldn't handle together.

Epilogue

Conal jumped as he heard the high-pitched squeak echo through the open door. Hastily dropping his pen on top of the contract he had been studying, he hurried into the adjoining room. He could see one small fist waving indignantly above the edge of the bassinet. A second later, a full-fledged bellow pierced the air.

"Hey there, Alastair." Conal reached down and gingerly picked up his tiny son. "No reason to get so riled up. I'm right here."

The baby stopped in mid-howl and peered nearsightedly at Conal as if considering the value of the statement. Apparently deciding it wasn't worth much, he began howling again.

"Shh." Conal gently bounced him. "Mom's with a client, and we don't want to disturb her. She's liable to think we don't know what we're doing."

Alastair howled all the louder, and Conal grimaced. "She might be right, too."

"How about a fresh diaper?" Conal carried the baby over to the changing table and carefully began unfastening his gown. The pediatrician might claim that at ten pounds Alastair was a good size for six weeks, but to him his son's tiny limbs looked fragile enough to break.

Finally managing to get the baby's diaper off, Conal awkwardly shoved a clean replacement under the baby. Before he could get it taped, Alastair wet it.

Conal gave his son a rueful grin. "You've got a lousy sense of timing, kiddo." Taking yet another diaper from the pile, Conal tried again, this time managing to get it on before anything happened.

Alastair, now that he was dry, stopped yelling and gurgled demandingly at Conal.

"What's the matter?" Conal asked as he cradled his son protectively against his shoulder. "You shouldn't be hungry yet."

Alastair gave a snort to show what he thought of that idea.

"You could be right, kiddo," Conal said. "I never had much patience with people who told me what I ought to be feeling, either.

"Tell you what, how about if I read a little bit to you while we wait for Mom to finish with her client?"

Alastair belligerently pushed out his lower lip.

Conal dropped a quick kiss on his downy head. "Sorry, son, but even with the best will in the world I can't feed you. Just don't have the basic equipment."

Conal hurriedly sat down on the rocker and, picking up the *Wall Street Journal* on the table beside it, began to read the editorials out loud. Alastair nuzzled his face against his father's shoulder, drooling onto Conal's crisp white shirt. Conal never noticed. He was too busy enjoying the feel of the baby's warmth against him.

"What on earth are you reading to him?" Livvy's laugh-filled voice broke into his thoughts.

Conal looked up, and the love he felt intensified a thousandfold at the sight of her bright face.

"The *Wall Street Journal*. Reading aloud to children is very important," he said seriously.

Livvy chuckled. "He hasn't made it to child yet. He's only a baby."

"But a very intelligent baby," Conal assured her. "I'm sure he understands most of what I say."

Livvy looked into Conal's serious eyes and bit her lip to keep from giggling. Conal was such a darling, and he was so endearingly earnest about Alastair. Everything the baby did Conal viewed as a new miracle created expressly for his enjoyment. He'd taken to fatherhood with a wholehearted enthusiasm. Much as he'd approached marriage.

Looking around the small nursery that joined their two offices, Livvy sighed in contentment. Conal had never even hinted that she ought to stay home with Alastair. Instead, he'd rented new offices for their thriving agency so they would have room for the baby, and he'd hired another account executive so they would both have time to devote to caring for the baby. Sometimes, at night, when she was nursing Alastair in the dark stillness, she would wonder what she had ever done to deserve such a fantastic husband.

"Have I told you lately that I love you?" Livvy asked softly.

"Not within the last half hour or so. We—" Conal jumped as Alastair let out a piercing shriek.

"I think he's hungry." Conal peered worriedly into the baby's red face.

Livvy chuckled as she took the baby and sat down in the rocker Conal had vacated for her. "I think he's just spoiled."

He's not the only one who's spoiled, Conal thought as he watched Alastair greedily filling his stomach. He couldn't believe that he had spent nine months terrified that he would be responsible for a baby. All that worry and all for nothing. Alastair was perfect. A replica of his mother. The love of his life. Conal reached out and gently ran the tip of his finger over Livvy's cheek.

She glanced up and smiled at him, and Conal felt as if life could hold no greater happiness than it did right at this moment.

* * * * *

Take 4 bestselling love stories FREE

Plus get a FREE surprise gift!

Special Limited-time Offer

Mail to Silhouette Reader Service™

3010 Walden Avenue
P.O. Box 1867
Buffalo, N.Y. 14240-1867

YES! Please send me 4 free Silhouette Desire® novels and my free surprise gift. Then send me 6 brand-new novels every month, which I will receive months before they appear in bookstores. Bill me at the low price of $2.90 each plus 25¢ delivery and applicable sales tax, if any.* That's the complete price and a savings of over 10% off the cover prices—quite a bargain! I understand that accepting the books and gift places me under no obligation ever to buy any books. I can always return a shipment and cancel at any time. Even if I never buy another book from Silhouette, the 4 free books and the surprise gift are mine to keep forever.

225 BPA A3UU

Name	(PLEASE PRINT)
Address	Apt. No.
City	State	Zip

This offer is limited to one order per household and not valid to present Silhouette Desire® subscribers. *Terms and prices are subject to change without notice.
Sales tax applicable in N.Y.

As seen on TV!
Free Gift Offer

With a Free Gift proof-of-purchase from any Silhouette® book,
you can receive a beautiful cubic zirconia pendant.

This gorgeous marquise-shaped stone is a genuine cubic
zirconia—accented by an 18" gold tone necklace.

(Approximate retail value $19.95)

Send for yours today…
compliments of ▼ *Silhouette*®

To receive your free gift, a cubic zirconia pendant, send us one original proof-of-
purchase, photocopies not accepted, from the back of any Silhouette Romance™,
Silhouette Desire®, Silhouette Special Edition®, Silhouette Intimate Moments®
or Silhouette Yours Truly™ title available at your favorite retail outlet, together with
the Free Gift Certificate, plus a check or money order for $1.65 U.S./$2.15 CAN. (do
not send cash) to cover postage and handling, payable to Silhouette Free Gift Offer. We
will send you the specified gift. Allow 6 to 8 weeks for delivery. Offer good until
March 31, 1998, or while quantities last. Offer valid in the U.S. and Canada only.

Free Gift Certificate

Name: _____

Address: _____

City: _____ State/Province: _____ Zip/Postal Code: _____

Mail this certificate, one proof-of-purchase and a check or money order for postage
and handling to: SILHOUETTE FREE GIFT OFFER 1998. In the U.S.: 3010 Walden
Avenue, P.O. Box 9077, Buffalo, NY 14269-9077. In Canada: P.O. Box 613, Fort Erie,
Ontario L2Z 5X3.

FREE GIFT OFFER   084-KFD
ONE PROOF-OF-PURCHASE
To collect your fabulous FREE GIFT, a cubic zirconia pendant, you must include this
original proof-of-purchase for each gift with the properly completed Free Gift Certificate.

084-KFDR2

SUSAN MALLERY

Continues the twelve-book series—36 HOURS—in January 1998 with Book Seven

THE RANCHER AND THE RUNAWAY BRIDE

When Randi Howell fled the altar, she'd been running for her life! And she'd kept on running—straight into the arms of rugged rancher Brady Jones. She knew he had his suspicions, but how could she tell him the truth about her identity? Then again, if she ever wanted to approach the altar in earnest, how could she not?

For Brady and Randi and *all* the residents of Grand Springs, Colorado, the storm-induced blackout was just the beginning of 36 Hours that changed *everything!* You won't want to miss a single book.

Available at your favorite retail outlet.

Look us up on-line at: http://www.romance.net   36HRS7

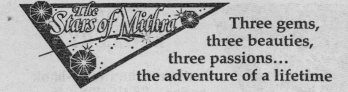

The Stars of Mithra

Three gems,
three beauties,
three passions…
the adventure of a lifetime

SILHOUETTE·INTIMATE·MOMENTS®
brings you a thrilling new series by
New York Times bestselling author

Nora Roberts

Three mystical blue diamonds place three close
friends in jeopardy…and lead them to romance.

In October
HIDDEN STAR (IM#811)
Bailey James can't remember a thing, but she knows
she's in big trouble. And she desperately needs private
investigator Cade Parris to help her live long enough to
find out just what kind.

In December
CAPTIVE STAR (IM#823)
Cynical bounty hunter Jack Dakota and spitfire
M. J. O'Leary are handcuffed together and on the run
from a pair of hired killers. And Jack wants to know
why—but M.J.'s not talking.

In February
SECRET STAR (IM#835)
Lieutenant Seth Buchanan's murder investigation takes
a strange turn when Grace Fontaine turns up alive. But
as the mystery unfolds, he soon discovers the notorious
heiress is the biggest mystery of all.

Available at your favorite retail outlet.